D0440806

HANNE ØRSTAVIK

LOVE

Translated from Norwegian by
Martin Aitken

a r c h i p e l a g o b o o k s

First Archipelago Books Edition, 2018

Library of Congress Cataloging-in-Publication Data
Ørstavik, Hanne, 1969- author. | Aitken, Martin, translator.
Love / Hanne Ørstavik ; translated from the Norwegian by Martin Aitken.
Other titles: Kjµrlighet. English
First Archipelago Books edition. | Brooklyn, NY : Archipelago, 2018.
LCCN 2017022875 | ISBN 9780914671947 (paperback)

Archipelago Books
232 Third Street #A111
Brooklyn, NY 11215
www.archipelagobooks.org

33614080786352

COVER ART: Edvard Munch

Distributed by Penguin Random House
www.penguinrandomhouse.com

This book was made possible by the New York State Council on the Arts with the
support of Governor Andrew M. Cuomo and the New York State Legislature.
Archipelago Books also gratefully acknowledges the generous support of
Lannan Foundation, the National Endowment for the Arts, and
the New York City Department of Cultural Affairs.
This translation has been published with the financial support of NORLA.

PRINTED IN THE UNITED STATES OF AMERICA

LOVE

WHEN I GROW OLD, we'll go away on the train. As far away as we can. We'll look out through the windows, at fells and towns and lakes, and talk to people from foreign lands. We'll be together all the time. And forever be on our way.

She gets through three books a week, often four or five. She wishes she could read all the time, sitting in bed with the duvet pulled up, with coffee, lots of cigarettes, and a warm nightdress on. She could have done without the TV too, I never watch it, she tells herself, but Jon would have minded.

She gives a wide berth to an old woman waddling along pulling a grey trolley behind her on the icy road. It's dark, the snow banked up at the roadsides blocking out the light, Vibeke thinks to herself. Then she realizes she's forgotten to turn the headlights on and has driven nearly all the way home in an unlit car.

She turns them on.

Jon tries not to blink. It's hard for him not to. It's the muscles around his eyes that go into spasm. He kneels on his bed and peers through the window. Everything is still. He's waiting for Vibeke to come home. He tries to keep his eyes open and calm, fixed on the same spot outside the window. There must be at least a meter of snow. Under the snow live the mice. They have pathways and tunnels. They visit each other, Jon imagines, maybe they bring each other food.

The sound of the car. When he's waiting he can never quite recall it. I've forgotten, he tells himself. But then it comes back to him, often in pauses between the waiting, after he's stopped thinking about it. And then she comes, and he recognizes the sound in an instant; he hears it with his tummy, it's my tummy that remembers the sound, not me, he thinks to himself. And no sooner has he heard the car than he sees it too, from the corner of the window, her blue car coming around the bend behind the banks of snow, and she turns in at the house and drives up the little slope to the front door.

The engine is loud, its sound fills the room, and then she switches it off. He hears her slam the car door shut before the front door opens, and he counts the seconds until it closes again.

The same sounds every day.

Vibeke shoves the shopping into the hall and bends down to undo her boots. Her hands are swollen from the cold, the heater in the car is broken. A co-worker she gave a lift home from the supermarket last week said she knew someone who repaired things like that on the cheap. Vibeke smiles thinking back. She hasn't much money, and what little she has isn't for cars. As long as it gets her from A to B, that's all that matters.

She picks up the mail from the table under the mirror. She feels stiff, though no more than normal after a busy day, and stands for a moment, rolling her shoulders and stretching her neck, arching back and releasing a sigh.

Now she's taking her coat off, he thinks to himself, and pictures her in the hall, in front of the mirror, hanging her coat on the peg and looking at herself. She'll be tired, he thinks. He opens a box of matches and takes out two, snapping them in the middle and wedging them cautiously in his sockets to keep his eyelids from blinking.

You'll grow out of it, Vibeke tells him when she's in a good mood. The matches are like logs, it's hard to see out. He thinks about his train set; he can't help it, it doesn't matter what he thinks about, a train always comes running into his mind, tilting into the bend with its whistle blowing, hurtling by. Maybe he could give her a face massage, he thinks, rub her cheeks and forehead the way they've learnt in gym class, it's supposed to be good for you.

She carries the bags into the kitchen, dropping the mail down on the table before filling up the fridge and putting some tins away in the cupboard. The engineer in the building department, the dark-haired man with the brown eyes, sat opposite her at the Culture Plan presentation. Her first project as new arts and culture officer. The cover was in full color, she'd insisted on it, an inspirational painting by a local artist.

She lingers at the table, drinking water from a glass.

It went off well, people came up afterwards and said how glad they were to have her aboard. Her presence spurred new visions, they said, opened their eyes to new potentials. The brown-eyed engineer had smiled at her at several points during the presentation. In the Q&A session he made a comment about being interested in extending interdepartmental collaborations.

She sweeps her hair away from her face, gathering it in front of her shoulder and smoothing it with her hand, pleased at how long it's grown at last.

He hears her footsteps on the floor above. Her shoes. Vibeke always wears shoes indoors. Sandals with a low heel. He removes the matches. He strikes one against the box without blowing it out, wanting to hold it as long as it burns. Skirt and lipstick for work. At home she changes into a grey jogging suit with a zip neck. Maybe she's changing now. *It's so soft inside, come and feel.* She gave him slippers when they moved in. Brought them home with her after work, one of her first days on the job, wrapped in flowery paper. She tossed them to him, he had to catch them in mid-air. Woollen slippers, ankle-length, with leather soles. A metal clip to keep them closed. If the clips aren't done up, they rattle when he walks.

Vibeke puts the glass down on the table. She looks out the window, at the darkness outside. The street lamps are on, lighting up the road between the houses. To the north, the road through the village joins the highway again. It's a kind of circle, she thinks to herself, you can drive in to the village, past the council offices and the shops, through the housing area, then pick up the highway again further up, follow it south, and turn off toward the village again. Most of the houses have their living-room windows facing the road. We need to address architecture, she thinks, the way it can bring things together. The whole village backs onto forest. She jots down some keywords on a sheet of paper: Identity, pride. Aesthetics. Information.

She goes into the front room. On the sofa is a grey woollen throw with white circles on it, the reverse is white with grey circles. She gathers it up and pulls her armchair over to the panel heater under the window. She takes a book, nonfiction, from the small, round table.

The book has a waxed cover, it feels pleasant to the touch. She smoothes her left hand over its surface before opening the pages. She reads a few lines, then puts it down in her lap, leans back, closes her eyes. She sees faces from work, people stopping by her office, how nice it's looking now. She goes through situations in her mind, repeating her facial expressions and gestures.

Jon stands in the doorway looking at her. He tries not to blink. He wants to ask her something about his birthday, tomorrow he'll be nine. He tells himself it can wait, she's asleep now. A book in her lap. He's used to seeing her like that. A book, the bright light of the floor lamp. Often, she'll have lit a cigarette and his eyes will follow the smoke as it curls toward the ceiling. Her long, dark hair fans out over the back of the chair, trembling almost imperceptibly. *Stroke my hair, Jon.*

He turns and goes out into the kitchen, and takes some biscuits from the cupboard. He puts a whole one in his mouth and tries to suck it soft without breaking it.

He goes down the stairs into his room again and kneels on the bed. He lines the biscuits up on the windowsill.

He looks at the snow outside and thinks of all the snowflakes that go to make a pile. He tries to count how many, in his head. They talked about it at school today. Ice crystals, they're called. No two are ever the same. How many can there be in a snowball? Or on the window pane, in a small speck of snow?

VIBEKE OPENS HER EYES. Through the big windows of the living room she can see the red tail lights of a car as it disappears down the road. She thinks of who it might be, her mind runs through everyone she knows. The engineer, she thinks, perhaps it was him.

She sits up and looks at the time, then goes out into the kitchen, puts some water on the boil and chops half an onion. When the water boils she takes the saucepan off the ring and drops some sausages in it along with the rest of the onion. She turns the radio on. There's an interview program on, but she doesn't listen. The voices make a kind of melody, changing back and forth. She tidies a dish away from the table. There are some bits left along the rim, some dregs of milk at the bottom. She's still got her short skirt on, she's had it for years, but it falls so becomingly around her bottom and thighs. The sheer stockings are a luxury she allows herself. Most people dress to suit the weather. Thick tights, often another pair on top that they take off in the toilets when they get there. Life's too short not to be dressing nice, she thinks to herself. I'd rather be cold.

She rinses the dish under the tap, using the washing-up brush to remove the bits that are stuck. Jon likes to eat when he comes home from school. Biscuits or cornflakes. Sometimes he'll listen to the radio while he's eating and forget to switch it off. More than once when coming in from work she's heard voices in the kitchen and thought they had visitors.

—

The interview program's finished, now they're playing a song and she knows the group, their name's on the tip of her tongue, but she can't for the life of her call it to mind. She feels the lure of sitting with a good book, a big thick one of the kind that leave an impression stronger and realer than life itself.

I deserve it, she tells herself, after how well I'm doing at work.

Jon sits down. The bed is next to the heater underneath the window. When he lies down he can feel the warmth all the way down his side. Up against the wall by the head of the bed is a set of shelves painted blue with various things on them: a radio, magazines, a roll of sticky tape, a torch, a water pistol. He presses a button on the radio and turns the dial until he finds some music. He tries to pick out the different instruments. Ghostly guitars, he thinks to himself. He heard someone say so once. Ghostly guitars.

He lies down on the bed and closes his eyes. He thinks that when he's not thinking about anything it must be completely dark inside his head; like in a big room when the light's switched off.

The name of the group comes back to her. Of course, she says to herself. A scene from a party after exams: another student, younger than she, his hair in a ponytail, they danced to that same song; he stood there with his arms around her from behind, grinding his hips in a way she supposed was actually quite vulgar.

She smiles.

She gets a packet of flatbread wraps from the cupboard, and a fork to pick up the sausages, pops her head around the door and calls for Jon, finds a mat for the saucepan and puts it down on the table.

She thinks of lighting a candle and rummages in a drawer, but they must have run out. What's he doing? She calls for him again, from the staircase this time. When he doesn't answer she goes down to his room.

He's playing basketball with some other boys in a dream. The sun's out, it's hot, and all his shots go in. He feels elated and runs inside to tell Vibeke. She comes quietly out of the kitchen. He starts to tell her, but the way she smiles is so strange he turns away to go to his room. At the elbow of the staircase he meets a woman who looks exactly like her. She whispers softly, coaxing him toward her. As he steps into her arms, a third woman comes up the stairs. Maybe she's Vibeke. He halts and stands there, without moving a muscle.

He wakes up and sees Vibeke standing in the door, the light all around her. She says the dinner's ready.

Jon goes upstairs after her. They sit down at the kitchen table. Vibeke turns the radio off. She sifts through the mail while they eat. Jon sees it's mostly advertising, from furniture chains and big supermarkets. There's a flyer with a caption that says funfair. He asks what else it says. Vibeke reads it out, there's a travelling funfair at the sports ground next to the council offices, they've got a spaceship ride and a gravity wheel. It won't be for you, she says. He asks if they've got 3D games. She doesn't know what they are. Space games, that sort of thing, he says, computer games where you're inside and you've got to steer your way through space and overcome all kinds of obstacles. Vibeke reads through the flyer again. It doesn't say.

He looks at her as she carries on eating and sifting through the ads. He hears the snap as she bites through the tight skin of her sausage.

Jon's ready for another one. They pile up inside his tummy like logs in the forest, there's always room for one more.

A path into the forest, from a long-forgotten place.
Find the path and follow, its ribbon yours to trace.
Past trees and hillocks wander, to a splendid castle old,
in whose halls three ladies fine you shall at last behold.
The prince they there await, if ever he should come.
A song they sing to pass the time, a lonely, plaintive hum.

"What was it like there?" she always wanted to know after the princess had been carried away to an unfamiliar castle. Tell me, Jon. He remembers sitting on her lap and describing to her the great, empty halls with their open windows and long, flowing curtains. Candles and soft rugs. You know just how I like it, Jon, she would say. I'm so happy in big, bright rooms.

He looks out the window. In the house across the road lives an old man. His driveway isn't cleared like the others because he hasn't got a car. Instead, he scrapes a narrow path through the snow with a spade. When he goes to the shops he uses a kicksled. It takes time, Jon's seen the way he stops and sits down on the seat to rest. He hasn't seen him out these last few days. It must be too cold. The path's almost buried again. The woman from the shop was there in her little car. She left the engine running as she highstepped through the snow up to the house. Jon watched her pass a pair of carrier bags through the crack of the door before cantering back down the slope to the car in the road.

Vibeke looks at her hand as she reaches out to take another wrap. Her fingers are long, her eyes trace the sinews on the back of her hand.

The inside air makes her skin dry, Spenol moisturiser is the only thing that helps. Then there's her nails. And her hair, too. The cold dries it out.

The town's not far from the village, yet it feels like an age since last she was there. She tries to remember when it was. Stop that, Jon. Just over a week ago. Saturday before last. The bookshop, of course. What else? She and Jon had cake in that no-smoking place. How awful it was, a plastic tearoom. That town needs a café with some thought-out design, it's like a house without a proper entrance. Stop it, Jon. It's been a while since I bought myself some clothes, she thinks to herself. She could do with a new outfit, she deserves it, with the move and everything. Stop screwing your eyes up like that all the time, Jon, you look like a mouse. She thinks of a narrow, plain skirt in beige she once saw a woman wearing at a seminar.

Jon looks at a picture on the wall by the window, an aerial photo of the village in a black frame. It was there when they moved in. He studies it while munching another sausage. The road is a straight line. Although it's an old photo and the colors have started to fade, there's no difference between then and now, apart from everything being newer when the photo was taken. He tries to think of who lives in the various houses, but the only ones he knows are where someone from his class lives. If he stares long enough at the photo they'll come out of the houses and start moving about like in a cartoon.

One of the boys in his class got a jet-fighter kit for his birthday two weeks ago. Jon wants a train set. Märklin. He only needs a few parts to start with, a length of track and hopefully an engine.

—

In his school bag is a book of raffle tickets for the sports club. When he's finished his dinner he'll go around the houses he can see in the photo to sell some tickets.

Vibeke gets to her feet, clears the plates and glasses and puts them on the counter. Jon kneels on his chair and leans forward across the table, she can see he's trying to harpoon the last of the sausages with his fork. He tells a funny story he's made up about a man who throws himself out a window and never reaches the ground. She doesn't think his stories have a point. He stabs at the sausage, lifts it up and breaks it in two, offering her half. She smiles. They always eat the last one the same way, on its own. He lingers, resting his weight on his elbows as if waiting for something. He tells her about a picture he's seen in a magazine of someone being tortured, a man suspended above the floor with a hood over his head. His arms are tied to a pole with some rope, he's been hanging there so long his arms feel like they're about to be torn from his body, says Jon. Can't you just go, she thinks to herself. Find something to do, play or something?

"It's good of you to think of those in pain," she says. "If everyone else did the same, the world might be a better place."

She reaches out and smoothes her hand over his head.

"Have you made any friends yet?"

His hair is fine and soft.

"Jon," she says. "Dearest Jon."

She repeats the movement while studying her hand. Her nail polish is pale and sandy with just a hint of pink. She likes to be discreet at work. She remembers the new set that must still be in her bag, plum, or was it wine; a dark, sensual lipstick and nail polish the same shade. To go with a dark, brown-eyed man, she thinks with a little smile.

Jon gets his school bag in the hall. He takes out the book of raffle tickets from the little pocket at the front where he puts his packed lunch. He puts on an extra pair of socks before doing up his grey boots. He puts on his coat and blue scarf. His woolly hat. He looks at himself in the mirror. He tries to stop it but he can't. He feels in the pockets of her coat. Among the receipts and an old bus ticket he finds some money. He shouts from the hall to say he's going out.

He opens the door and stands there on the step for a moment. He can feel in his nose when he breathes in how cold it is.

JON PASSES ALONG the length of Vibeke's car. He pauses, wedges the book of raffle tickets tight between his knees, scrapes a handul of snow from the trunk of the car and presses it together in his palms. It's a poor snowball, dry as powder. He blows it from his mittens, then claps them together, a crisp, loud report. Sounds become so weightless in the cold. Everything does. As if he were a bubble of air himself, ready at any moment to float into the sky and vanish into the firmament.

He takes the raffle tickets in his hand, crosses the road and walks up the little path the old man has cleared in the drive. The snow crunches under his feet. There's a lean-to by the front door with fire-wood stacked up under the pent roof. Snow has blown in between the logs. The outside light is switched off. Jon finds the doorbell. He presses it, but can't hear a sound. Everything's so still, he thinks to himself. But then the old man opens the door, so abruptly it makes him jump.

"Would you like to buy a raffle ticket?" Jon asks, holding out the book. "It's for the sports club."

The old man looks at him, his eyes then darting toward the road. It's been a while since a car came by and it's too cold for people to be going about on foot. He gestures for Jon to come inside. He closes the door after him and goes through another door into the house itself. Jon stamps the snow from his feet and follows on.

They enter a living room with a small kitchen area attached. On top of the kitchen counter is a small television set. There's a black-and-white film on with the sound turned off. The old man shuffles over to a wood burner and bends down stiffly on one knee. He puts a log into the fire, wraps his hand in his sweater and opens the vent to a crack, then turns around and smiles at Jon.

"That should keep it going for a bit. Can't have people freezing when they come to see the old crow."

A rocking chair by the window is still faintly in motion. He must have been sitting there when the doorbell rang, Jon thinks to himself. Maybe he saw me coming.

"The sports club, you say." The old man wanders over to the counter and pulls out a drawer. He asks how many tickets Jon's got and what they cost. Jon tells him. He takes out a wallet and says he'll buy them all. He writes his name in the book and puts a ditto mark in curly brackets on all the stubs. It takes him a while. Jon glances around.

Three oval photo frames hang on the wall above the rocking chair with old portraits in them, the photos are the kind that are blurred at the edges as if the people in them are fading away. In a corner of the kitchen area is a fishing rod. Jon wonders if it's a fly rod. Last year Vibeke had a boyfriend who said he would teach Jon to fish with a fly. Just the two of us, he told him, guys together. He took out a map to show him where they would go, showing him where the river ran and describing the various pools. There, he said, you'll catch a big one there. He looked up at Vibeke with a smile. But then one day he was gone. Jon hadn't even heard them argue.

The old man turns toward him, handing him the raffle book and the money.

"You're new here, aren't you?"

"Yes. We came four months and three days ago."

Jon puts the money and the book of stubs in his bag. He feels glad.

"And already out and about selling tickets, eh? They know how to put you to work in that sports club."

Jon says he's only just joined so he can start skating.

The man's hair is white as chalk, long, thin, and untidy. His face looks flushed, Jon thinks to himself, as if he just woke up.

"Let me show you something," he says.

"What is it?" says Jon.

He tries not to blink.

"You'll see. I'd nearly forgotten all about it, forgotten altogether."

He opens a door and flicks a switch. A lightbulb goes on, fixed directly to the wall. Jon sees a flight of stairs leading down into the basement.

Vibeke goes to the bathroom and stares into the mirror. She can tell from the way she looks it's been a good day. She feels glad and full of bounce. At one with herself. A tiny crystal twinkles from the right wing of her nose. She winks back. My lucky star. She picks up a brush and bends over until the long, dark mane of her hair nearly touches the floor. At first she brushes with care to remove the tangles, proceeding then with gentle, sweeping strokes from the scalp. She tosses her head back when it's done. She wants her hair to look like a cloud caressing her face. She looks in the mirror. It lacks volume, and wayward strands strive toward her forehead. I could go to the library, she thinks to herself. Normally she keeps the library until Saturday, and today's only Wednesday, but she's already run out of books to read. She decides to take a bath first and wash her hair, treat herself.

Jon follows the old man down the stairs. They're steep, the man takes one step at a time and there's a thick rope he holds on to at the side like a banister. At the bottom they go through a little passage, a mat of artificial grass covering the floor. The place smells rank and strange, Jon thinks it smells of soil. The man stops at a door at the end. He turns toward Jon, his hand on the handle.

She takes off her clothes while she runs her bath. There's no bubble bath left in the bottle. She takes a cotton bud from a box on the shelf and removes her nail polish with some remover. She waits until it's nearly full before turning the tap off and climbing cautiously into the tub, water sloshing over the side. She feels the goose pimples as they appear on her skin, her nipples harden and a tickle runs down her spine. She lowers herself gently down. Such bliss to immerse the body in hot water, she thinks to herself. Bliss, in every respect. And then she lies there, motionless, savoring every second.

"You'll like this," the old man tells him.

There's a daybed up against the wall, and shelving full of old wooden boxes from floor to ceiling. The room smells of dust and mold. Jon thinks maybe the man's got a collection of old model trains, the first electric ones in Europe. He feels a need to pee. The man crosses the floor to a shelf, pulls a box out from the middle and dips his hand inside. A leather dog collar and a metal chain hang down from a hook on the wall.

"Have a look at these," says the man.

He turns around, holding up a pair of brown skates.

"Handsewn. My father gave them to me."

He offers the skates to Jon. Jon steps forward and feels the stiffness of the leather between the tips of his fingers; the skates quiver, the old man's hand a tremble.

"Luxury in those days," the man says. "Handsewn leather on iron blades. No one in the village had anything like them. I won the Kalottløpet in these, the young men came from all over, from Rovaniemi, Utsjok, Neiden, and further inland, Russians. On the lake it was, the Storvannet. A thousand meters. Before Stalin and Hitler and that whole hellish mess. On black ice, when the water freezes before the snow."

Vibeke rubs the shampoo into her hair, her fingers moving in little circles like at the hairdressers. She closes her eyes to shut out all external stimuli, wishing to be present inside herself, sensing the world from within. She remembers a dream she had, a man saying: "You look gorgeous.' They were standing at the foot of a carpeted staircase, in front of some mirrors with gilded frames; there were doors, deep red, leading off to some bathrooms. They were at a party, the party was going on at the top of the stairs; there were people, lights, a babble of voices. The music was loud, but downstairs was quiet. The man had come through a door and noticed her and said: "You look gorgeous.' She felt so excited and leaned forward to give him a hug, and he kissed her gently on the cheek. Then he turned and left through a revolving door, in his dark suit and white shirt. He didn't have a coat on, just a thin woollen scarf draped around his neck. She stood there for a moment, looking at herself in the mirror. Smiling. Elated. That was the good part. The rest wasn't worth thinking about. All of a sudden the party was over. The lights went off, the staircase was no longer there. She saw that she was alone in a public toilet, a stench of urine filled her nostrils, the floor cold against her stockinged feet. She went through the revolving door where the man had gone, and came out onto a wasteground of asphalt and ice, a single street lamp shining just ahead. There was a wall, and in the wall was a gateway; she walked toward it, thinking it would lead out to a road.

At least the beginning was good, she says to herself. A party would be fun, though. She could have one here in the house, invite the people from work. Break the ice, get herself a network. She imagines the living room done out with candles and cascades of flowers. The gleaming eyes and peals of laughter. In her living room. She could do a lovely written invitation with a quote from a poem.

She rinses the shampoo from her hair with the shower head. The pipes shudder as she turns off the tap. She sweeps the shower curtain aside and looks at her body in the mirror, its image blurred by steam. What would they drink from? She won't have enough glasses for that many people. She'll have to buy some in town on Saturday. She's seen some with tinted stems and bowls. Then again, perhaps that would be overdoing it. She decides to find some others that are pleasing and simple, and of good design.

JON GOES BACK OVER the road, back to the house. Stepping inside he makes sure the door shuts behind him, there's ice on the sill. He pulls off his mittens and drops them in the little white basket in the corner. He goes downstairs to his room with his coat still on, and puts the bag down with the raffle book and the money in it from the old man. On his way out the man cut him a little chunk off a dried ham hanging from a hook in the vestibule. He puts it down on his desk.

He stands there a moment and looks around him, at his poster of the Milky Way and the planets, the blue and green stripes of the wallpaper. He feels relieved to have sold all his tickets, he'd been dreading having to go around with his book. He wonders what to do now. He tries not to blink but can't stop himself. He puts the green water pistol in his back pocket and goes back up the stairs. He tries to see how quick on the draw he is in front of the mirror.

It's hot with his coat on inside, he's sweating, but he won't take it off. He wonders what he looks like when he blinks, but he has no way of knowing. Maybe if someone took a picture of him he'd be able to see. Vibeke emerges from the bathroom. She's naked, with her hair in a towel. He looks at her, then tries not to see. Oh, there you are, Jon, she says. I thought you were out. She carries on into the living room, he hears her put a CD on, the click of the buttons, the little pause before she presses play. It's the same song she listens to in the mornings before she goes to work. She calls out to him as if he were far away: Jon, have you seen my body lotion?

—

Jon takes aim at himself in the mirror. He holds the pistol steady in both hands, elbows pressed against his trunk as he fires. What does a body look like when it's full of holes? He thinks of jelly babies and chocolate cake with light-colored filling, not dark like the last birthday he was at. Behind him in the mirror he sees Vibeke come from the kitchen with the body lotion, still naked, holding the bottle up with a smile so he can see she found it. She waltzes back into the living room and turns up the sound. She likes to stand there while she rubs in her lotion after her shower in the mornings. But she doesn't normally shower in the evening. He wonders if it's to save time on his birthday tomorrow.

He feels a draft now that he's standing still. It's from the front door. They should have it insulated, with weather stripping and draft excluders like he's seen in other houses. He sticks his water pistol in his back pocket and puts on a different woolly hat. Vibeke needs to be on her own so she can get things ready. If he's out while she's baking the cake it'll be more of a surprise, he thinks to himself. He goes out. Reaching the road, he wishes he'd put his mittens on, but he won't go back.

VIBEKE CALLS FOR JON. She can't find yesterday's newspaper, there was an article in it the people at work said was good. In her right hand she holds a cigarette. He doesn't answer. She saw him only a few minutes ago. She turns the little lamp on above the sofa and checks to see if the papers have fallen down behind. Most likely he's doing something in his room. She picks up her bag and takes it with her into the bathroom again, stubbing her cigarette out in the sink. She puts on her bra, sits down on the toilet seat and finds the bottle of nail polish in her bag. She unscrews the top and considers the deep red polish on the little applicator brush, sensing an urge to find out what it feels like against her lips. Soft and cold, she imagines. She applies the nail polish to her toenails, stretching her foot out to admire after each is done.

Jon walks toward the center of the village. The street lamps leave pools of light on the ground, he moves from one to another. He hears music and a distant rumble of machinery, he thinks it must be the funfair that's open. He quickens his stride. On the empty stretch near the nursing home he stops to break off a stick and writes his name with it in the snow. Jon. He stares at the letters before rubbing them out again, not wishing to leave a trace. He throws the stick as far as he can into the trees, blows into his hands and walks on.

As he comes around the bend he sees two girls skating in the road further on. Their hair is long and trails behind them in the air when they twirl around. Girls' skates, he thinks to himself. For twirling.

He thinks of his own with their long, shiny blades. The girls carry on skating as he approaches. He sees they've been practicing some movements they perform together. They've got short skirts on over their quilted pants, trying to look like figure skaters on TV, he thinks to himself. The road is completely white. The snow banks here aren't brown and grimy the way they are in the town, there aren't enough cars here for that. He leans back against a post a short distance away and watches. He tries not to blink. He puts his hands in his trouser pockets to keep them warm. His trousers are tight, his hands press flat against his body. He wonders if he looks like a cowboy in a film, standing against the wall outside the saloon. A cigarette dangles from his lips and his eyes narrow to slits as he peers through the mists of smoke he blows from his nose and mouth. One of the girls skates up to him. She stops and stands still on her blades, he can see her balance is good. She asks him if he wants to play Kick the Can. Her cheeks are so cold she has trouble pronouncing it properly. They laugh.

Vibeke blows on her fingernails and flaps her hands in the air. She wonders what time it could be. It's Wednesday, wasn't there something on TV she wanted to watch? She can't remember what it was. She drapes a dressing gown cautiously around her shoulders and goes into the living room, pressing the remote with the pad of her finger. Of course, that was it. It's already started. British soap someone at work called it. Even so, the meticulous English is nice for a change, instead of drawling American.

She lies back on the sofa, resting her head against a cushion. She feels the tie of her dressing gown slip down the inside of her thigh.

—

Her left hand finds the cigarette packet on the table without her having to look.

"It's too cold," the other girl says. "Anyway, there's got to be more than three."

She's got white boot covers on, with a zip down the middle. They look soft and warm, Jon thinks. He's standing between them. They're taller than him with their skates on.

"Have you got skates?" the first girl asks, the one who came up to him.

"Yes," says Jon. "I'm on the team at the sports club. I've just started, so I'm not that good yet, I haven't had enough practice."

He tells them about the old man's skates. They've never heard of the Kalottløpet. He feels himself blinking again.

They step to the side of the road to let a car come past. The smell of exhaust lingers on the ground.

The other girl says her elder brother's the best skater in the whole region. He's twelve years old. The first girl laughs and says they're best at everything in that family. Jon cups his cold hands in front of his mouth and blows.

"You can borrow my mittens if you want," she says.

She points up at the nearest house.

"I've got some others at home."

She hands Jon the mittens. They're red. He puts them on. They feel a bit tight. He can tell they're new because the furry lining inside hasn't gone lumpy yet. The other girl says she's going home. She pulls a knit cap out of her pocket and puts it on with the flats of her hands,

—

the tips of her mittens sticking up above her ears. Jon thinks it makes her look like a rabbit.

They walk toward the driveway of the house. When he turns around, the other girl is already some way down the road. He can see she's not skating, she lifts her feet as if she had shoes on.

HE HAS TO WAIT in the vestibule while she asks if it's okay to bring someone home. There's a puddle of melted snow on the green flooring from the boots dumped at each side. Just like at ours, he thinks to himself. Normally he brushes the snow from his boots on the step, but it doesn't matter how hard he tries there's always some left to make a puddle. The walls of the vestibule are grey. The door leading in to the hall is frosted glass with brown-painted woodwork. He hears voices, a rush of water in the pipes, then someone turns the tap off and it stops. Jon recognizes a smell but can't remember what it is. He hears someone coming again. Through the glass he sees the blurred outline of the girl, her red sweater, a hand reaching out toward the door handle in front of him.

The house smells of firewood burning in a wood burner. A dry smell. They go up the stairs. There are some doors leading off the landing. She opens one, switches the big light on and lets him go in first. It looks like she shares with someone else, there are two beds. The window is straight in front, facing the forest to the rear of the house. He goes up to it. A pair of patterned curtains hang down at each side. He looks out. He sees how the light from the windows of the house extends toward the trees. He thinks the dark tree trunks in the white snow are like lines of charcoal on a piece of paper. The further away they are, the closer together they seem. Eventually they recede into black. She asks why he keeps doing that with his eyes all the time. Jon says he doesn't know. He turns toward her, he says he tries not to, but he can't help it. The girl blinks a few times. It's tiring, she says. I don't think about it, says Jon. My aunt's got a glass eye, says the girl. She kept looking through keyholes when she was little, only one day my dad was on the other side, he stuck a screwdriver through the hole to stop her spying. Feel like a game of Othello? Before he can say anything she gets the box out from under one of the beds. They sit on the floor with the board and all the black and white counters in the middle.

The program's finished now, the credits are rolling. Vibeke sits up, she'll have to get a move on if she wants to take some books out before they close. The brown eyes. She sees them everywhere, whenever she blinks, like the little stars you see after looking at a bright light. She wonders what it must be like to live with an engineer. What are they interested in? She goes into the bedroom and puts some clothes on, sporty and casual, nothing that might look calculated. In case she bumps into him at the library, stranger things have happened, there aren't many places to go here. She wonders what section he'd be browsing. Science. Crime and thrillers. Travel. Biographies. Perhaps even poetry. She blow-dries her hair in the bathroom, bending forward, proceeding from the roots to the ends. When she's done she tosses her head back and looks in the mirror. Success or fail? Not bad at all. She smiles at herself and rummages through her cosmetics. Powder, would he go for powder, she wonders, and dashes around the house, picking up the books to take back and dropping them in a bag.

She goes out into the vestibule, buttons her coat and studies herself in the mirror, pops her head back into the hall and calls out to Jon. She looks at her reflection again. She decided on hardly any make-up at all. He's not answering. She calls again and glances at the time, less than half an hour before they close. He's started going to bed on his own now, she's not even allowed to come in and say goodnight. She thinks of his eyelashes, almost white. She moves her head from side to side, checking her hair in the mirror, the way it falls so softly about her face, her scalp still warm from the time it took to dry it. She snatches the keys from the little table, picks up the bag with the books in it and smiles at herself in the mirror again before opening the front door and stepping out.

—

THE CARS ARE PARKED up in rows outside the community center. Some people are sitting inside them because of the cold, rolling down the window to chat with someone they know in the car next to them, engines idling. Vibeke pays no attention. She slams her door shut and checks the handle to make sure it's locked. The funfair, she thinks to herself. That's what they're here for, there's hardly ever a soul in the library. People should make use of it more often. It's such a pleasant place to come, with potted plants and nice posters on the walls. She goes toward the entrance, the library's in the community center basement. Someone whistles but she doesn't turn to look.

It looks dark behind the glass doors. There's a sheet of paper with the opening hours on it stuck to the other side of the glass. Vibeke realizes she's mistaken. Late opening is Tuesdays and Thursdays. On Wednesdays they close at three. I forget this place is so small, she says to herself. She drops the books through the return slot. It almost hurts to let go, the way they splay out in a heap on the floor. It's like leaving some people of whom she's grown fond.

She leans back against the wall and lights a cigarette, not knowing quite what to do now, having had a bath and everything. Her eyes follow a car as it skittles away, snow kicking up from its wheels. She looks across at the festoon of colored lights at the entrance to the fair. They shine so brightly against the darkness of the sky, as if to tell everyone how irresistible they are. Our day's Carnival, Vibeke thinks to herself.

Maybe I should go in and have a look. Maybe there's someone who can tell fortunes.

"It's my birthday tomorrow," says Jon.

"Let me guess, you'll be eighteen," the girl says with a laugh.

Jon has the upper hand, his black counters are all over the board. The girl has given up and isn't taking it seriously anymore.

Vibeke goes in through the fairground entrance. A reveller bumps into her, braying something unintelligible and carrying on oblivious. She stops and looks around. The fair's set out in a kind of horseshoe, tombolas and amusements around the edge, rides in the middle. The spaceship ride she read about rumbles along with half-empty cars, a young girl squeals and the music pounds, driven by the same generator that powers the rides.

The tombolas are small trailers with open hatches along the side. At one stands a woman with long, white hair reaching down to her waist. Vibeke thinks it must be a wig. She's holding a yellow plastic tub full of tickets. Her hands are covered by long, white gloves edged with imitation fur, her cape is white too, and on her feet she wears tall, white boots. The woman looks straight at her as she walks past. Then new customers make her busy. Her make-up's overdone, Vibeke thinks to herself, she ought to make more of an effort.

The girl rummages in a carrier bag hanging behind the door. She takes out a cassette and goes over to the tape recorder on the window sill.

"This is really good. I like to listen to this when I'm relaxing."

She turns the flat tape recorder on its side so the sound can come out into the room, puts the cassette in and switches it on. He sits down

---

35

on one of the beds. She sits on the other and looks at him, then lies down on top of the cover with her face turned toward him. He can tell from her eyes that she's listening to the music. They look at each other. He feels it in his tummy, the train as it comes hurtling. He's standing in the middle of the track and it's coming straight at him, it's going to run him down, the engine's as big as a five-storey house. But instead it whisks him up and takes him with it. Now he's crouched in a cradle at the front of the train, carried along, gently and unperilously, the wind in his eyes, but that doesn't matter, because behind him is the train, and it feels like snuggling up to a warm, living creature.

The music sounds Indian, or Chinese, he's not sure. He leans back against the wall and closes his eyes. He's driving a train in China, the track runs along the top of the Great Wall, up and down it goes, and up and down again, with a view of white-painted mountainsides and a winding river far away in the distance. He opens his eyes again and feels how tired he is.

She seems to be asleep. He thinks she looks like someone from Asia. It's to do with her eyes, the taut skin around her lips, the way her mouth seems to merge into her face. Or maybe it's her face that merges, he thinks to himself, seeping toward her mouth, vanishing into the slit between her narrow lips.

Vibeke goes over to a cabinet where you put a coin in to steer a kind of arm that shoves prizes down into a hatch. There are various prizes you can win, like colored fountain pens with a little flashlight at the end of the cap, imitations of old-fashioned lipstick cases to put refills in, with fake gold and a little mirror on the side, a variety of wristwatches, some see-through plastic boxes containing silk scarfs and ties. The prizes are all laid out on a bed of bright yellow cellophane. Little lights built into the top of the cabinet shine down on the cellophane from different angles, making it twinkle and shimmer. Besides the cellophane there are marbles of many different colors. From a distance the marbles make the cabinet look like it's full of diamonds, Vibeke thinks, and smiles at the thought. She puts a coin in and tries to steer the arm toward a lipstick case. The prize is just about to tip over the edge into the chute, but then the arm goes up again. Five marbles fall into the hatch instead. She puts them in her pocket.

Jon thinks of birthdays he's seen on TV. The family wakes the birthday boy or the birthday girl up in the morning, they come into the room with a cake with candles on it and their arms laden with packages. The parents kiss each other. But that's in America. You hardly ever see what's in the packages. He thinks of the train set he's seen in the shop, its smart red and grey, the engine with its detachable snow plow at the front. The best carriages have actual doors so you can put passengers in. Jon's the conductor, he wears a uniform and sells his tickets cheerfully to everyone. Then he's the engine driver, driving the train through tunnels in the fells, across tawny plateaus, through narrow green valleys with thin, glittering streams. Vibeke stands waiting at one of the stations. He stops to let her on. He blows his whistle so everyone can hear. She sits at the front with him in the driver's cab, she smokes and looks out at the light and the landscape. Jon speaks into the microphone and orders some tea.

"I like your hair."

She looks up and sees a man in dark-blue overalls. He works at the fair, she's seen quite a few like him in the same thick workwear. He asks if she'd like a smoke. His hair is a shock of thick, blond curls, his face a bright smile. Vibeke thinks he looks nice. A simple type, more than likely, but why not? She smiles back and says yes, she would. He leans against the cabinet and offers her the packet with a long, slender hand. It's a full packet. Maybe he doesn't actually smoke, she thinks to herself. She pulls out a cigarette. He takes one too and puts it between his lips. He puts the packet in the left-hand breast pocket of his overalls before patting for a lighter. He finds one in a back pocket and lifts his hand to give her a light. She looks at his nails, cut to the quick. His eyes latch on to the stud in her nose, she tries to work out what he thinks of it. He smiles again, his eyes are big and sad and happy all at the same time.

"Did you win anything?" he asks as he lights up.

Vibeke shows him the marbles. They lie in a cluster in her palm. At the center of each is a kind of colored propeller, encased in gleaming glass.

"I remember losing my best marble," he says. "I dropped it under a grate outside the main door at school. In the second year, I think it was. I could stand there and look at it every breaktime, but the grate was too heavy to lift and I was too shy to ask the caretaker. I thought it was the end of the world."

She studies him as he looks out over the fairground. A cheer goes up at the shooting gallery, a group of young men dressed up in Superman outfits throw their arms around each other and slap each other's backs like they were celebrating a goal. Vibeke thinks it must be a stag party. They both smile.

—

"It's cold standing here," he says, taking a drag.

"Yes," she says. "It is."

She wants to say more, but she doesn't know what. Not that she thinks they have anything much to talk about, she just feels a bit sorry for him, that's all. This is his life, traveling around with a funfair. She puts the marbles back in her pocket, circulating them between her fingers, and stamps her feet a couple of times to keep warm. The man takes a final drag of his cigarette then drops the end at his feet, mashing it into the snow under the sole of his boot.

"Got to get back to work," he says with a nod toward the space-ship ride.

"You staying around for a bit?" He looks at her with his head tilted slightly to the side, a look of sincerity in his eyes. He smiles again, and she answers: "Maybe."

She watches him as he goes back to the small wooden shed where the controls are housed. A queue has formed, a pair of teenage girls keep shoving each other in and out of the line. He goes in by a door around the back, she can just make him out inside, he has to bend down to take the money through the low, glass-fronted hatch. When there's no more queue, before he starts the ride, he leans forward and looks out at her. He waves and makes a face. Monkey in a cage. She can see him laughing.

She realizes there's no ferris wheel and supposes the fair to be too small for one. Maybe this is a winter version and they've got more in the summer. In the middle is a merry-go-round with colorful motor-bikes and sports cars. Some smaller children have been on a few times,

—

but apart from them its customers are few and far between. It goes too slow, Vibeke imagines. She looks down at her feet. Her boots are quite new. She feels her nylons under her trousers, they pinch her thighs in the cold.

THE CUDDLY TOYS SIT crammed together on shelves all the way up to the roof of the tombola stall. At the top are some giant teddies, pink, green, and grey. The wall behind is covered with what looks like silver foil. The woman dressed in white stands on a little platform that runs along the front of the stall, surveying the fairground. After a moment she comes over in Vibeke's direction, descending from the platform by a pair of steps. Vibeke wonders whether to walk away, but the woman's already holding her yellow tub out toward her.

She stops right in front of her with only the tub between them. Vibeke sees her face is powdered white, her lips too. She picks a ticket and pays the woman what she says they cost. Each ticket comprises three little windows. The sign outside the stall tells her each window hides the face of a playing card. To win you've got to get three the same, but there are prizes for other combinations too. She takes off her right glove and opens the windows with the nail of her thumb. The nail is a deep, glossy red; she'd quite forgotten. She can see she hasn't won anything and tosses the ticket into a cardboard box at the side of the trailer. Between the stalls she can see some other trailers parked around the back. That must be where the workers live, she thinks. What a sad life it must be. Beyond, the distant lights of a car heading south along the highway illuminate the sky above the trees. Her eyes follow their path.

"Hi there," a low voice says behind her.

—

Vibeke swivels around. It's the woman in the white wig again. She holds out her tub and gives it a little shake. Vibeke buys another ticket.

THERE AREN'T AS MANY people on the fairground now. Some have gone into a five-sided, red-and-white striped tent where it says they've got heaters inside. Apparently there's a sideshow of some kind about to start. Vibeke takes off her glove and massages her lips with her right hand. Music was coming from the big loudspeakers on the trailer roofs, but now it's stopped. She's not sure how long it's been quiet. A few minutes, perhaps. She tries to think back. Or maybe just a few seconds, the pause between two songs. She hears the sqeaky crunch of her footsteps in the snow. The music starts again. The different loudspeakers don't seem to be entirely in synch. Maybe it's just the tape that's a bit worn, she thinks. She stamps her feet in time to the music and feels like dancing, taps a cigarette from the packet and lights up.

He emerges from the shed by the spaceship ride. That didn't take long, she thinks to herself. He's carrying something under his arm as he comes toward her. He looks small among the rides.

Vibeke, she says to herself. Pull yourself together. Not a fairground worker, surely.

"Having fun?" he says, and stops in front of her before adding: "Well I'm done for the night anyway." His voice is soft and he looks straight at her as he speaks. It feels as if the moment expands, taking on some newer, deeper dimension than she was prepared for. She looks at his boots in the trampled-down snow, her gaze passing over

—

his dark-blue overalls, pausing at the yellow ferris-wheel patch at the thigh, continuing upwards to his eyes. His eyes are intense, she thinks to herself. A strong gaze.

"Up for a coffee?" he asks, and smiles again.

She realizes how cold she is, her feet especially are freezing. Thoughts pass through her mind like a slideshow. A travelling fairground worker. But it's only a coffee. She smiles and says yes.

They pass some pinball machines on a raised platform as they walk toward the trailers on the outskirts of the fair. The trailers are made of a kind of corrugated metal. Aluminium, perhaps. Or steel. She's not sure, she's never seen any like them before.

She can't hear any traffic from the road. It's getting late. He walks in front and she notes how straight he holds his back. She likes it, it's a sign of self-esteem, a man who knows who he is.

He stops and turns toward her, taking a packet of chewing gum from his right trouser pocket. He asks if she wants some. She shakes her head. He puts the cash box down in the snow while he takes off the wrapper. He glances up at her and smiles before pressing the stick of gum down against his tongue. The gum is brittle and breaks. He laughs, and Vibeke laughs with him. He takes her hand and gives it a squeeze, and his eyes look at hers.

"Hi," he says softly, then bends down to pick up the cash box before they walk on.

Vibeke looks up at the stars.

The trailers are bigger than they look from a distance. In front of each door is a pair of steps or a stool. The snow has already been trampled down to a path, as if the fair had been here for some time. Most of the trailers have got aerials on them, one's got a big satellite dish and the TV on inside. She sees its blue flicker behind the thin curtain, the shadow of a man as he gets to his feet.

He holds the door open for her. She steps up onto the little stool, gripping the door frame with one hand. Inside, she sits down on a folding chair and starts to undo her boots. She looks up at him. He pulls off his overalls while reading something on a little poster. The warmth inside the trailer makes her realize how cold she is, her thighs, calves and throat are freezing.

She follows him inside, sitting down where he indicates. They're in the living area, there's a grey table and an angled sofa in flecked green. Above the sofa there are windows on all three sides. The curtains are drawn. A kind of jungle pattern with splashy parrots.

"What a lot of room in here," says Vibeke. "It's like a little house. I can't remember the last time I was inside a trailer. You don't need much more than this. It's minimalistic and functional at the same time."

She looks up at the ceiling above the table. There's a poster stuck to it with tape, a blue-green sky with the orange circle of a sun in the middle.

He peers into a cupboard in the kitchen area, searching for something, the light striking his face from below, throwing his eyes into shadow.

"These open kitchens really are super. You can be doing the cooking and still be part of the conversation," she says.

—

"Looks like instant's all we've got," he says, filling the kettle with water.

She says instant will do fine. A few simple touches would work wonders here, she thinks to herself. All it needs is for someone to sew some cushion covers in matching colors, pull down those hideous curtains and put some new ones up that aren't as fussy, plainer ones to let in the light. And of course get rid of that awful poster on the ceiling.

There are some books on one of the shelves above the windows. She tilts her head to read the titles. Fiction by writers she's never heard of. Men.

She looks at him. All of a sudden his features seem to emerge and become clearer to her. His face expresses reflection, she thinks to herself. There's a classic quality about him. He triggers pleasant images in her mind: the two of them together on an endless beach, it's winter and they're the only people there; she runs along the shore and he gazes at her, seeing everything she contains, intelligent and warm.

He plugs the kettle into the socket above the counter and switches it on, opens a cupboard and takes out two mugs that chink as he puts them down.

She thinks how handsome he is.

JON DREAMS HE'S WALKING home with Vibeke. They turn into the big yard at the back of the building they lived in before. It's been snowing, the white of the ground is bright against the darkness of the yard. They go toward the far entrance. Vibeke goes first, her movements are normal, it's as if she can't hear that everything around them is so still. Inside the entrance the mailboxes have been vandalized, the lids hang from their hinges. It seems like the whole building has fallen into disrepair, no one lives there anymore and there's no more mail to deliver. Vibeke opens their own mail box as if she hasn't noticed. The entire row of mail boxes almost comes away from the wall with a scraping sound. Everything goes so slowly. He hears footsteps on the stairs. He was sure the building was empty, but now someone's there. They stand still and wait. It's the downstairs neighbor, he says the soldiers are on their floor now, in the flat across the landing from theirs. He whispers the words and creeps back upstairs again. They follow him without speaking, climbing the staircase as though nothing was wrong, perhaps more quietly than usual, though not silently by any means. The door of their flat is open. They go inside. The place is dark. A uniformed man sits eating in the kitchen. The man is his father. Light shines down on him from a bulb above the table. All the neighbors are gathered around, standing or seated. The man munches the fat cheese, the slices of ham. The butter. The white bread. He cuts thick wedges from the cheese. It's all the food they've got. They've been saving it, eating only sparingly. He piles layers of ham on top of his cheese. They watch him as he eats. They watch in silence. He eats and eats, and as he chews the food he tells sad stories about his life that make him cry.

Jon stirs, his mouth is dry. The light is on and he sits up. The girl is asleep on the other bed. She must have dropped off too. He tiptoes over and stands there looking at her. She's pulled the cover up, her right hand still clutching it under her chin. He touches her hand. Her skin feels soft and warm. Her hair is almost as fair as his, curled by the perspiration on her brow. There's a ticking noise and he glances around. It's the tape recorder, it's still on play after the tape has run out. His finger presses stop. The walls of the room are painted pale orange. A poster hangs above her bed, tall, leafy trees with a path leading among them, winding away into the forest. At the head of the bed hangs a small cross, next to the curtain some jewellery on a nail; he sees a little heart of grey stone on a chain. Someone has stuck stickers on the bed frame. On the floor between the two beds are some comics. He bends down and looks at the covers, there are some he hasn't read. He sits down on the floor and starts reading while he waits for her to wake up.

Vibeke curls her hands around her mug as if to keep them warm, but there's nothing in it yet. The man from the fair is in the shower. She doesn't know his name. I must remember to ask, she tells herself. She thinks he might be a foreigner, there's something different about him. The nose, she thinks. Maybe he's Jewish. But he doesn't have an accent.

The kettle switches itself off and she gets up to put the coffee in the mugs. There are some teaspoons in a jar on the counter, she uses one to measure the amount. The cold spoon in her hand makes her think how tidy the trailer is, too tidy almost, and clean. There's a photo stuck to the cupboard over the counter with a drawing pin. It shows some people posing together in a huddle by a table set for dinner. They've all got moustaches, drawn in with what looks like charcoal.

"My family," he says behind her.

He's pulled the curtain at the rear of the trailer slightly to one side and stands towelling his hair.

"Christmas dinner last year. My sister always takes some pictures with the self-timer and sends us all copies. Says it makes her feel like we're a family."

Vibeke sees him now, to the left at the back, next to an elderly man with a beard. His hair is shorter in the photo, he looks younger. She wonders how his sister can send him letters when he's always on the move with the fair. Most likely they've got an itinerary so people know where they're going and when. But if they do well in one place maybe they stay longer, in which case there'd be a knock-on effect and the itinerary would go to pot.

"I made it a bit strong," she says, and sits down again.

"That's all right," he says, looking at her as he combs his damp hair back.

He sits down on the sofa on the opposite side of the table and bends over his coffee, almost dipping his nose in it. Mm. Then he leans back against the cushions, studying her and smiling, as if this

—

is all he's been waiting for. It feels nice, she thinks to herself, being together like this. She feels an intuitive sense of knowing him. The person he is. The things he needs. The direction he's going in life.

"It must be such a freedom, traveling from place to place, meeting new people. Nothing to cart around apart from what can go in a trailer," she says.

"Well, it's not all roses."

His voice is warm. She feels his eyes upon her again, it's like his gaze is so powerful it lifts her off the ground and keeps her floating in the air.

"Roses aren't as harmless as you might think."

She almost whispers.

He smiles again. He's a man for me, she thinks. Her body senses it to be true, the insight is physical. The body can be trusted.

She feels a draft from the window behind her. The air in the trailer is muggy after his shower, the windows are probably all steamed up behind the curtains. The cold air nips at her upper back and neck. She lifts her shoulders to her ears and folds her arms around her chest. Her lips shudder. Brrr. He says he's got a sweater somewhere. He's responsive to signals, she thinks to herself and laughs. He leans forward and rummages in the storage under the sofa.

"This cold spell's been going on for ages," she says. She wishes she could think of something to say that would bring them closer, open things up a bit more. He pulls a woolly blanket out.

"Here," he says, rising to his feet and handing it to her across the table.

Stooping under the low ceiling, he knocks his mug over in the process. He swears, spitting the words harshly as the coffee runs over the edge of the table onto the floor. She can see the dampness of his brow at the hairline.

Jon puts the last of the comics down and gets to his feet. He needs the toilet. He looks at her again. She's still asleep. He can see the whites of her eyes. She must be waking up, he thinks. He stands quietly and waits for a moment, but she doesn't stir. He thinks maybe her eyes are always like that when she's asleep, with the whites showing. He feels an urge to wake her up so he can tell her. Then abruptly she opens her eyes wide and looks at him.

"I need the toilet," he says.

She closes her eyes again. Jon can tell she's gone back to sleep. He wonders if she was asleep when she looked at him too.

The woolly blanket helps. Vibeke watches his strong, slender hands as they snatch wads of paper towel from the roll and lay them out on the table and floor. The coffee seeps through and turns the paper brown.

The bedroom door creaks as he opens it. He can't hear any other sounds in the house. The landing is dark. He thinks the people he heard before must have switched the lights off and gone out. Or maybe they've gone to bed. Vibeke must be wondering where he is. He can see some carrier bags and a heap of clothes by the railing at the top of the stairs. He pulls his waterpistol from his back pocket and holds it at the ready in his right hand. He listens, crouching forward before edging toward where he thinks the toilet must be. Cautiously he

—

opens the door, only to find it's another bedroom. This one has two beds in it as well, one by each wall, a rag mat in the middle under the window. One of the beds is still made. A little lamp shines above the other one. It looks like someone's just been lying in it, the sheets are messed up, and on the floor next to it, in the light of the lamp, is a book with its pages open.

He closes the door. At this very moment in time, someone, somewhere, is being tortured. Maybe there's a torture room in this house. Maybe someone's a prisoner here and it's his job to find them and get them out. He doesn't know where to begin. He opens another door that looks like a cupboard, only with a proper handle to turn. He finds the switch inside the door and turns the light on. There, under the sloping wall, is a toilet with a wooden seat.

He draws rings in the bowl with his pee. It smells different here than at home. He watches the water as it flushes away, thinking suddenly of the light of summer, the way he can lie in his bed and look out the window, the sky completely white, feeling himself dissolve.

"We're moving on tomorrow," he says, stirring coffee granules into another mug of hot water. Vibeke asks where they're going. He says they're off west first, south after that.

"It's too cold here," he says with a smile.

Vibeke nods.

"You get used to it," she says.

He asks what she does.

"Arts and culture officer in the local authority," she says. "I've only just started. The people are nice and there are some very exciting challenges in an out-of-the-way area like this. Identity and community are important concepts to theme if we're to counter the drift toward the urban areas, and culture's a very appropriate instrument in that respect."

He looks at her as he listens, smiling when she's finished. She feels like touching the stubble of his beard with the tips of her fingers, smoothing her hands over his face the way she does with the covers of her books.

"Apart from that I like reading, that's my way of traveling," she says. "I was actually going to the library tonight, only it was closed."

She falls silent for a moment.

"So I came here instead."

He gazes into the curtain next to her. She feels like they share something now. It feels like pushing a boat from the shore, the moment the boat comes free of the sand and floats, floats on the water.

THE PHONE RINGS SOMEWHERE in the house. It keeps on ringing, no one answers. Jon follows the sound, down the stairs to the ground floor. Light seeps into the hall through the glass door leading out to the entrance porch. By the wall is a bucket of water, next to it a cloth wrung dry. He locates the phone, it's on a set of drawers underneath a mirror. He lifts the receiver while looking in the mirror and says hello. One side of his face is in the light from the entrance porch. At first he hears a low hum of voices, as if from some very big room, like the departure hall of a small airport, he thinks to himself. Then a man starts talking. He says they're doing a survey. He asks what brand of soap the household has used most often during the last month and rattles off a list of names. Jon says he doesn't know, he doesn't live there. The man asks if he can speak to someone who does. Jon says there's no one in. The man says goodbye and hangs up, Jon hears the dial tone, a faint hum, as if the man had called from some faraway place.

"Who was it?"

The girl is standing on the stair. The phone must have woken her up. He sees her in the mirror, her face looks puffy.

"Why did you say there was no one in?"

"I thought you were asleep," he says.

He puts the receiver down.

"You could have woken me up."

"I suppose so."

"Why didn't you then?"

"I don't know." He tries to remember what thoughts passed through his mind when he heard it ring. "It was only a survey, someone wanting to know about soap," he says.

He looks at her in the mirror. She doesn't say anything, her eyes are fixed on the phone. He feels himself blinking again. He tries to stop. Her hair hangs down over her shoulders, it looks almost luminous in the dim light, and her red sweater looks black.

He thinks she looks older now than in the bedroom. She could be fifteen or seventeen.

When she speaks again it feels like they've been standing there for a long time in silence. She asks him if he wants some cocoa.

He follows her into the kitchen. She turns the light on at the switch above the counter. It flickers before going on. Jon leans against a cupboard while she gets the milk and sugar and the cocoa out. He thinks about the train set. Maybe he'll get it tomorrow. *Next year you can make a list and wish for something big, because this year it's going to be things you need. But soft packages are nice too, though, aren't they?* Vibeke says she likes to keep a promise. The train set is at the top of his list. Vibeke's bound to have seen the list he left on his desk.

He thinks about the train and the model landscape in the shop window in the town, the lights that change from green to red and back again, the little figures on the platform. He remembers a boy in a blue padded coat outside a shop.

She uses a metal whisk in the saucepan. They don't speak, all they do is stand next to each other, watching the whisk as it smoothes the

—

dark brown paste at the bottom. She adds the milk and they watch again as it heats up.

She puts the saucepan on the table and ladels cocoa into the cups. They sit across from each other, slurping with chocolate moustaches.

"Where did you live before?"

"Farther south. We had to move."

"Did you go to a big school there?"

"Yes," says Jon.

She asks how you make friends in a big school. He thinks about it.

"I'm not sure," he says after a while. "It just happens, that's all. In class, or in something after school. I was in a role-playing club, but they only played historical games with Vikings and stuff. I'm more into science fiction."

"Are your parents divorced?"

"Yes. My mom had to get away," says Jon. "She was too young to be tied down. I was still little, so it's normal for me."

"I've seen you on the school bus," says the girl.

Jon tries to work out if he's seen her too. He can't remember her face, but he remembers someone giggling near the back one day. He turned around and saw two girls, one with fair hair, the other darker. He wonders if the fair-haired one might have been her.

"What class are you in?" he asks.

"Four," says the girl. "It's boring."

She starts telling him about the classes and what teachers they have and how dull she finds it all. He looks out at the snow-covered road and the house diagonally opposite. It's dark in all the windows. Jon thinks it must be night now. He sees some headlights approach, and a glimpse of the vehicle as it drives past and away, a van with black paintwork. Jon wonders what would happen if it stopped outside the window. He imagines it's got flames painted along the sides so that when it goes fast it looks like the front wheels are on fire and the flames are trailing behind. He's seen a Matchbox car just like it. He pictures a thin man dressed in black getting out of the driver's seat, uncorking a bottle and knocking back a swig while staring straight into the kitchen where Jon's sitting with his cocoa.

She switches the TV on. The first music video shows things from a distance at first, in fine colors, then the camera zooms in so you can see what everything looks like close up. A fruit bowl, for instance, with some sliced melons in it; what looked like seeds from a distance are actually wriggling, white maggots.

Jon sees the cocoa in his cup has formed a skin. The girl turns up the sound. They're still at the table, slouching a bit now, with their heads resting against the backs of their chairs. He studies her. The two small bumps under her sweater. Her mouth hangs open as she stares at the screen. He tells himself it's late, time he was going, and lowers his feet to the ground so he can stand up. He thinks Vibeke must be finished baking now, she'll be sitting in the kitchen with a cigarette. He hopes she's left the bowl for him to lick.

Without taking her eyes off the screen the girl says he can't go yet. There's one more he's got to see. She's waiting for it and he can't go before he's seen it too.

He tells her about something that happened at the fair. Vibeke pictures him in her mind, they're in the forest together, it's summer and he's walking in front of her, breaking off twigs, tasting a berry. He turns around to face her and smiles, silently, as if in a film, and more than just once. There's a clearing in the trees and a bright light slanting down on him, and he becomes a white fleck in her mind, like when you look straight at the sun.

He laughs, obviously at something he's just said. She smiles back and before thinking about it she's risen to her feet and says she needs to use the bathroom. She dizzies from standing up so fast, for a moment the smells inside the trailer seem almost overpowering, the air's still muggy from his shower, and his strong-smelling deodorant and the fact that she can't see out of the windows makes it feel like her face is being pressed into her skull.

The walls of the tiny bathroom are covered in postcards from different places. She pulls her pants down and sits down on the toilet. She sees a card from the town they lived in before they moved here. The picture's been taken at night and she can hardly recognize the place. Someone's drawn a map and stuck the cards up according to the geography. She follows the land north. There's a postcard approximately where the village is, an aerial photo. You can see the slack curve of the road running between the little buildings, the council offices, the school that's now been closed down, a stretch of the highway. The sports ground where the funfair is has been marked with a red cross. She finds her own house. Someone else's car is parked in the driveway.

"The fair's been here before," she says when she comes back out. He's lit up a cigarette.

"Probably," he says. "They've got various routes they follow, but usually they keep to the same places."

He pauses.

"First time for me in this place."

He utters the words abruptly while stubbing his cigarette out. He hasn't finished smoking it; she sees the way his hand trembles slightly. He stares at her for a moment, unsmiling and rather nervously, she thinks. She wonders if he suffers from anxiety. It's like he's asking her something, or asking himself. She tries to convey with her eyes that she wants to be there for him and listen.

He says he's hungry.

"I've got bacon and eggs, if you want some?"

"Yes, that'd be nice," she says.

He squats down and opens a small fridge underneath the gas cooker, taking out eggs, bread, bacon, and butter. He seems smaller in here, she thinks to herself. Thinner. She thinks of him curled up at one end of the sofa with a book, the stillness, the affection she feels for him when he reaches up to get a frying pan from on top of the cupboard.

—

THE GIRL'S TURNED the sound up even more. It's loudest in Jon's left ear, he feels like his head's one-sided. He stands at the window in the kitchen and watches as a dog trots up the driveway of the house over the road, sniffing its way up to a bin behind some bushes. Nearly everyone's got one the same here, a white dog with black or brown markings. They run around loose, Vibeke says it's a shame for people who are scared of dogs, they hardly get out. It disappears behind the bushes, popping into view again on the other side and going up to the front door. The outside light's the only one on. The dog enters its beam. The door stays shut. There's no one in, no one calling or whistling for it. It carries on around the corner until he can't see it anymore. A few seconds later it comes out on the other side of the house. It stops and lifts its leg before scampering back through the powdery snow to the road.

He turns to the TV again. Now there's a video on with a lot of people dressed in black plastic rubbing themselves against each other. One of the women has a hole in her jacket so you can see her titties, and safety pins through her nipples. One of the others comes over and starts pulling on them. Jon thinks it must hurt.

He must have felt a draft because he swivels toward the door. A woman and a man are standing there. They're standing next to each other with their hands at their sides like an old photograph. All of a sudden they start to move, as if they ran on batteries.

The woman asks the girl to turn the sound down. She says hi to Jon and they sit down at the table. He thinks it must be the girl's parents. They chat to each other about someone he doesn't know. The mother gets up and fetches two cups, then pours the rest of the cold cocoa into them. She hands one to the man and drinks from the other one herself. Jon thinks they look older than Vibeke. They're not in any hurry. The man's hair is messy. He flicks through a sales brochure for some farm equipment while talking to the girl's mother. His hands are big and tanned even though it's winter.

"It's on, look," the girl says, pointing at the TV. "About time. This is great."

She turns the sound up again so they can hear. Her mother gets to her feet and goes over to the counter. She takes a loaf of bread out of a plastic bag. She keeps talking to her husband as she cuts some thin slices off using the bread slicer. Jon finds her cheerful.

The smell of cooking mingles with the scent of the deodorant he used a short time ago. The bacon smells good, Vibeke realizes how hungry she is.

"You've fried eggs before," she says, smiling as he cracks the eggs into the pan. He says the fair employs an odd-job man who cooks for them too, so he doesn't bother that often himself. He gets the plates and the cutlery out while he's talking, and two glasses, a mat for the frying pan. He leans across to put them on the table. Vibeke places her hand on the table top. Her slender hand with its deep-red nails, pale and delicate, such a contrast to the masculinity of his own.

He picks up on her movement and lowers his face to hers. She sees his eyes are grey with a touch of green, and feels his breath against her right cheek. His lips part as he leans closer, his tongue wet with spit.

Perhaps he chews tobacco. Behind his head a light bulb dangles from a cord in the ceiling. It swings backwards and forwards. It seems to go faster.

The girl's mother heaps the bread onto a plate and puts it in the middle of the table. She opens the fridge and gets out some liver paste, some jam, and two cartons of milk.

"Jon," he says when she asks him his name. She smiles.

She asks if they've been to the fair, she says there were a lot of cars parked outside the community center when they went past. She remembers they saw someone they knew, one of the neighbors, he looked so funny. She does an imitation and laughs so much her belly jiggles up and down. Jon had forgotten all about the fair, now he remembers it was where he was going when he went out. He looks across at the girl, she looks back at him. He thinks she looks annoyed, as if he stopped her from going to the fair. He looks at her mother. She's turned back to the counter now and is humming a little song.

Jon counts the rolls of fat on her back. Five. The girl's father's on the chubby side too. He thinks it must be nice for them to have such a thin daughter. Her parents have dark hair, but the girl's hair is nearly white. Just like mine, Jon says to himself.

"Wait," says Vibeke.

"What for?" he says.

"The eggs. They'll burn."

"Forget the eggs," he mumbles, a laugh almost, and bears down on her. She twists away, her right hand finding the handle of the frying pan. She nudges it onto the back burner. He straightens up with a thin smile and runs his fingers through his curls. He turns the heat off while studying her. His eyes send tingles through her body, injecting her with energy. Who said grey eyes don't gleam, she thinks. He caresses her with his eyes, and she soaks it up.

She leans her head back and pulls some strands away from her face, neatening herself, beholding him with her entire being. She breathes out. It was close, but she's glad she stopped it. It doesn't feel right. Not yet, not here. He's such a handsome man and when they succumb to each other it should be in a place that becomes them. Somewhere more befitting.

Her cheeks are flushed. She laughs and feels attractive and buoyant. Her blushing will only make him more excited, she thinks to herself, it forms a basis for later; he can see me glowing.

There's a knock on the window behind her. She turns around and pulls the curtain aside. It's the woman in the white wig. Her face is pressed against the pane, peering in.

Jon looks up at the wall by the kitchen door. There's a picture of a peacock on it next to the light switch. It's made from a wooden panel painted black with tacks hammered in to form the shape of the bird. Jon thinks of Jesus's hands as the nails were hammered into his palms. Silk threads in all sorts of colors have been woven between the tacks. The bird's outline is different layers of orange.

The girl's mother sees Jon looking.

"Our eldest did that. There's two more in the living room, but they're just made up, not meant to look like anything. He did them when he was in school."

She sits down at the table and butters a slice of bread, smiles and passes the plate to Jon.

—

"What does he do now?" Jon asks.

She looks at the man, who glances up from reading some text underneath a picture of a tractor.

"What's he say? What he's doing now?"

The girl and her mother chuckle at how he wasn't listening.

"He moved down south and we didn't hear from him for a while. He's working on a farm now."

The man looks down at his brochure again while the woman carries on.

"He met a girl in a cafeteria. He was waiting for a bus, she worked there and they got chatting. They had a little girl last year. They live together on the farm, all three of them."

She gets up while still talking and pulls out a drawer full of papers and photographs. She rummages about a bit before finding a photo she hands to Jon.

"Sara," she says with a nod at the picture. "After a singer, they said."

Jon sees a little red face in a pale green blanket, in the middle of a great big bed. He feels tired. He hands it back and looks at the others she keeps finding in the crammed drawer.

The woman in the white wig has drawn her cape around her, clenching it together at the throat. Vibeke thinks she must have climbed up onto a pile of snow under the window, their faces are level, not even half a meter from each other. She wonders if she saw anything. The curtains were drawn, but the light inside is bright. She tries to look unruffled. There can't have been much to see anyway, we've hardly gotten to know each other yet. The woman stares at her with a half-smile, Vibeke's not sure whether to smile back. Then her eyes latch on to him. He's standing behind Vibeke, so close she can feel his warmth against her back. They stand there for a moment, then the woman turns and walks off.

Jon asks what time it is.

"Eleven," the man says right away, without looking up.

Jon thinks it must be later than that, but he doesn't want to say so. The girl gets up and turns the TV off. The room goes quiet. She yawns and stretches her limbs. Jon sees a glimpse of her bare skin as her red sweater rides up.

"I'm off to bed now. See you," she says to Jon.

She leans over the table and kisses her father on the cheek. Her pants stretch tight across her butt, Jon thinks she looks like a boy.

Vibeke stays seated, holding the curtain open with one hand. It seems darker out now, as if the lights have been turned off. She leans forward and presses her cheek to the cold pane, watching the woman as she strides off in the direction of the rides. A bit further on she stops at another trailer, opens the door and goes inside.

Vibeke turns back to the table. She asks who it was. He lifts the frying pan and divides the charred food onto the two plates with a knife. She sees him open his mouth and close it again. He looks at her, then throws up his hand in an empty gesture, still holding the knife.

"She works here."

He puts the frying pan down on the mat on the table.

"I bought a raffle ticket from her earlier on," says Vibeke. "She seems rather weird. A bit unhinged, even. It's like she's searching for something."

"You might not be far off there."

He smiles as he punctures the yolk with his knife, cutting the egg both lengthwise and sideways, and lifting the food into his mouth with his fork. Vibeke doesn't fancy anything now.

"It can be okay in the short run, but after a while people like that just get on your nerves.'

His cheek bulges with food as he speaks. He looks at her as if wanting her to confirm what he's saying. She nods.

She listens for sounds from outside, voices, footsteps, scraping.

All she wants is to tell him how good-looking he is.

Everything is still, apart from the bacon crunching between his teeth. Then a generator kicks in somewhere and starts to hum.

JON STANDS BY THE CHAIR. He ought to go now that the girl has gone to bed, but he likes it here. There's a scorch mark on the table from a saucepan. The girl's father has switched to leafing through the local paper, her mother stands with her back to them at the counter, dividing some leftovers from a pan into some small plastic bags. I'm not from these parts either, she says to Jon. She tells him she's from Finland, further south, but her husband's related to practically the whole village so she feels at home here anyway. Jon watches her as she works. It must be okay for him to stay if she's still talking to him. Her fat body remains still, only her arms move, steady and calm. When the bags have been filled she twirls them and twists a thin fastener around each. She smiles at him. She takes the bags with her out of the kitchen. Jon hears a door creak on its hinges, then the sound of heavy feet going down a staircase. He supposes they've got a freezer in the basement. The girl's father turns the page of his newspaper without looking up. Tomorrow Jon will be nine. He feels it in his tummy, he feels it wanting to come out of his mouth too, but he doesn't say anything. He smiles. He hears the girl's mother come up the basement stairs again.

Vibeke thinks he seems troubled now. Not at all like before. She wants them to talk about something important.

"How about a whisky?"

He's standing at the open cupboard. Before she can answer he's got two glasses in one hand and a bottle in the other. He puts them on the table and moves the dirty dishes over to the counter. He's eaten her portion too.

"See you," says Jon. The girl's father says something he doesn't catch in reply. On his way into the hall he walks straight into the mother. He feels her big belly against his arms, her heavy breasts hang level with his mouth. He tries to stop blinking as he mutters goodnight.

When he gets to his feet after doing up his boots he feels dizzy. He steadies himself with his left hand on the wall. Maybe there's something wrong with his heart. The front door isn't locked. He goes out and closes it behind him, giving it a push to make sure it's properly shut.

The forest behind the house is dark. There's a pisshole in the snow at the corner of the house, Jon wonders if the dog he saw earlier might live here. It's not the dog, it's the hair, Vibeke says whenever he asks if they can have one.

His hands are cold already. He puts them in his trouser pockets. He thinks about the girl and the whites of her eyes as she slept.

He goes down the driveway to the road. He thinks he'll look out for her on the bus tomorrow, maybe he'll tell her then.

ONCE IN A WHILE can't harm, Vibeke tells herself, holding the glass while he pours. The whisky is golden, like distilled fire.

"Besides, the weather's been so cold," she says out loud.

"Exactly," he says, raising his glass before knocking back its contents and pouring himself another.

They each light a cigarette. He picks up the cash box and says he needs to balance the takings while he's still got a clear head. Vibeke leans back against a rolled-up duvet in the corner and puts her legs up on the sofa. She rests her glass against her chest, watching him through the smoke she exhales. He sits with his head bent over the money. He hums a tune, tapping out the rhythm with his foot. Vibeke thinks how agreeable he is to be with. Easy-going and unconventional at the same time. She listens to the sounds drifting in from outside, voices in high spirits, cars revving up and speeding off. She feels chosen, privileged to be here in this little trailer with such an unusual man. Suddenly he starts to sing in full voice, a jazz song, an upbeat standard phrase with a hectic chorus, the table is his drum kit, his fingers a cymbal flicking against his glass.

She smiles at him.

She feels warm, perhaps he's turned the heater up. Not wanting to perspire, she takes her sweater off. Underneath she's wearing a wide-necked top in blue and grey, a blend of silk and flax. She closes her eyes and listens to his song, glad that he feels so uninhibited, so relaxed and sociable.

—

Jon curves out of the driveway into the road. He walks in the middle now that there's no traffic. There are some spent fireworks in the snow. He picks one up and puts it in his pocket, thinking he can investigate what's left when a firework has been used, there's a microscope he can borrow in the science room at school. He feels himself blinking again. Sometimes he forgets he's doing it. He tries to see how many paces he can walk in between each blink. He hears the sound of a car and turns his head to see, it's coming from the village and going fast. He steps to the side and jumps up onto the bank of snow. He looks at the car as it goes past. It's red. He thinks he's seen it before, but he can't remember where. It was a man behind the wheel, with close-cropped hair and a long cigarette in his mouth.

He stops singing and she opens her eyes. He's sitting up straight now after counting the money. He looks at her. His gaze is deep and unfathomable.

"All done," he says, and claps his hands together, a loud report in the air. "Now to find somewhere with a bit of life."

She hadn't thought of them going out. She pictures them together on a dance floor with the lights down, he holds her close and whispers sweet nothings in her ear. She wonders why the idea hadn't occurred to her. It just goes to show the way we can free each other and release our respective potentials, she thinks to herself.

"Yes, let's," she says, her interest quickened. "It'll be nice."

He looks a bit surprised. Didn't he think she'd want to? There's a lot he doesn't know about me yet, she thinks with a smile.

He puts a thick woollen sweater on and wriggles himself into a leather jacket, looking in the mirror as he pulls a knit cap down over his ears. His eyes look even bigger when his hair isn't falling into his face. She feels a stab of emotion at the thought of him going away. There's something in his eyes she needs to investigate, something she wants to get close to. She gets up and goes past him to the front door where she left her coat and puts it on. When she's ready she turns and looks up at him, leaning back against the wall next to the bathroom. She's waiting for something, listening to the voice inside him.

He opens the door and they step out.

It's cold.

She hears a loud voice from inside a trailer, a man sounding angry.

She lingers a few meters behind as he knocks on one of the other trailers. An older man comes to the door, small and bony, she can't see his face properly because he's standing in the light from inside, it shines through his thin, white hair. She sees the cash box change hands and the two men exchange a few words, their voices a murmur. He stands with his weight evenly distributed between both legs, he's tall and yet he has to look up at the older man, who's standing a couple of steps higher. The older man takes a wallet from the pocket of a coat hanging inside the door, he opens it and gets something out which he gives to her man. She can tell from their jangle it's a bunch of keys. The man in the door looks at her. She smiles back at him. She can hear children's voices inside, a boy and a girl. It sounds like they're playing a game.

SHE FOLLOWS HIM ACROSS the empty fairground. He moves elegantly as they pass between the rides, she thinks. Nimbly, like a man in form. He walks almost too fast for her. Because of the cold, she supposes; he wants to get to the car as quickly as possible.

He veers left outside the fairground entrance and goes over to a boxy, dark-green vehicle. Vibeke doesn't know what they're called. It looks like a jeep. Army surplus, perhaps.

He glances at her before unlocking the door. He gets in, leans over the seat and opens her door from the inside. Vibeke steps up onto the running board and climbs in. He looks at her as he turns the ignition. It's like he's asking her something, but she can't figure out what. She smiles to put him at ease. She wishes he could be a bit clearer. She likes people to be straight about what they think, so you know where you are with them.

The engine starts first try. They sit for a moment and glance at each other before he puts his arm over the back of her seat, twisting around to look through the rear window as he reverses out, turning the steering wheel with the flat of his hand.

It's a very powerful car. Most likely they use it to pull trailers with, she thinks to herself. She pictures the big chunky tires, they must have a good grip on the road. She leans back in the seat and finds it to be soft.

He drives out through the parking area by the community center and the supermarket, past the council offices. There's no one around, though still a few cars parked here and there. People will be talking about the fair tomorrow, Vibeke thinks to herself. This is their idea of culture. This is what they want, but when was the last time there was a jazz concert in the church or a reading by an author at the library?

He turns out onto the highway, accelerating through the gears, the heater blowing out hot air. He leans forward and turns the radio dial until finding a channel with some choice, upbeat music. She buckles her seat belt. He starts humming again. She looks out at the road, her eyes following the reflective marker poles. There's very little traffic on the highway at night, she thinks. Coming from the southerly direction in the dark it can look like someone inexplicably put lighting up on an empty stretch of blacktop. It's not until after a few hundred meters of lit-up road that you come to a sign and the turn-off to the village, and realize that people actually live here.

They leave the illuminated stretch behind them and everything outside the beam of the headlights is immediately dark. She doesn't know what song he's latched onto, it's a little snippet, he keeps humming it over and over, even with the radio playing something else. She feels they should sing something together, like they used to in the car when she was a child. She closes her eyes. He's a good driver, she thinks to herself, the way he negotiates the wide bends is so effortless. She wonders if he can tell how contented she feels.

"Tell me something," she says.

"Like what?"

"The first thing that comes into your head."

He doesn't say anything.

In that case she'll have to help him. She thinks if she keeps on giving, then eventually she'll get through to him.

—

"I remember a rhyme from a story," she says. "It's one of the loveli-est things I know."

"Really."

"It goes like this:
Far, far away there's an ocean,
in the ocean is an island,
on the island is a church,
in the church there's a well,
in the well swims a duck,
in the duck there's an egg,
and in the egg—'
She almost chokes up:
"In the egg is my heart."
The words come out a whisper.

The voice on the radio is talking about a new film that's premiering at cinemas in the cities. It all seems so remote. The car and the road and the beam of the headlights are the only things that exist. She looks at him, he's staring straight ahead, unsmiling, severe almost. Perhaps what I said touched him and now he's trying to grasp it, she thinks to herself. She feels like stroking his hair, running her fingers through his thick, unruly curls.

She reaches out and does so.

He gives her a look in return.

She looks out at the road ahead, at the banks of snow shoved aside by the snow plows, at the marker poles, the forest. Everywhere she looks there's snow and more snow. They come to a yellow sign and she can see there's still a bit to go before they reach the town.

—

It feels like it isn't cold anymore, Jon thinks, though he knows it can't be true. It's always colder at night. The road is empty. It looks bigger now than in the day, wider somehow, it makes the way home seem longer. He hears a brisk padding of feet behind him and wheels around to see the dog from before. It stops and sniffs at something on the ground. Jon feels the blood pound in his head. There can't be anything wrong with his heart after all. He pats his thigh and calls to the dog. It lifts its narrow head and looks at him for a second before going back to its sniffing. He gathers up some snow and tries to form a snowball. It's as hopeless as before, only the snow's too hard now. His hands are freezing, he throws it into the air. The dog comes bounding, excited by the icy shards as the snow hits the ground and disintegrates. He manages to call it over to him and pats it on the neck. It wags its tail. When he starts to run the dog follows.

THE FRONT DOOR IS locked. Jon is out of breath, his skin feels clammy underneath his scarf. He searches his pockets for the key. Normally he keeps it in the front pocket of his trousers where he can feel it against his thigh. But it's not there. It's not in any of his other pockets either.

He doesn't want to wake Vibeke up. He thinks she must have locked the door when she went to bed, maybe she got tired of waiting for him after baking the cake. He feels in his pockets one more time then presses the bell. He hears it ring inside the house, a long, determined trill. He pictures Vibeke's face, without make-up, her thin legs below her pale-blue dressing gown. She'll give him that tired look of hers. Maybe she won't let him in, maybe he'll have to stay out until morning now, for having been out so late. He didn't want to wake her, he'll say, only he couldn't find his key.

No one comes. He presses the bell again, longer this time, his index finger holding the white button in. The lit-up recess for the occupier's name is empty, he can see the wiring behind the cover.

He swivels around and leans back against the door. The key must be on the table in the living room, he thinks to himself, and pictures his keyring, Donald Duck encased in transparent plastic; when he makes it twirl it looks exactly like Donald is keeping his eye on him.

He thinks the space in front of the house has got bigger too. Then he sees the car's gone. Vibeke isn't in. Maybe something's happened.

An accident. Vibeke doesn't like driving in the winter. Here it's winter all the time. She's crashed and maybe now she's paralyzed and will have to sit in a wheelchair. Maybe no one's found her yet and she's bleeding to death. Or maybe the car's about to burst into flames and she's going to die from the pain. He tries to imagine how much it hurts when your skin is on fire. No one's found her and she's all on her own. He feels himself blinking, he screws up his eyes and presses his fists against his sockets, as if to press them into his skull. Maybe if he presses them far enough in they'll dangle about inside his head and never find their way back to the hole where they can see out. Then I'll have to have my birthday at the hospital, he thinks, with my head wrapped up in white bandages. Vibeke will have to bring him his presents and the cake there. Maybe she's run out of something for the cake, he thinks. Eggs, maybe, or flour, and now she's popped out to borrow some. That'll be it. She forgets things all the time, she says she's like a doddering old professor who thinks so much he can never remember anything. She'll be back soon if that's what's happened, he tells himself. He should have known. If it hadn't been his birthday in the morning she wouldn't have needed to go out again. He realizes his toes and the front of his thighs no longer feel cold. He stamps around in the snow outside the door and jumps up and down. He tries to think what to do while he's waiting. He hopes she isn't angry.

At a distance up ahead they see the illuminated interior of a parked car. A little pocket of light in a shoulder on the left-hand side of the road. He slows down, they exchange glances. Vibeke wonders at first who might have stopped here in such an empty place surrounded by forest, then why they would turn the interior light on, making them visible to anyone driving by.

"Do you believe in UFOs?" he says with a chuckle.

"Perhaps they've broken down," she says. She can hear how unlikely it sounds, anyone breaking down so close to the town would surely go for help. As they drive by, Vibeke glimpses two men in the front seats, their heads lowered as if they were looking for something on the floor. They're in uniform, Vibeke thinks maybe they're security guards on their way from one job to another. But by then they've left them behind.

"Good thing they were occupied," he says.

"What do you mean?"

"Police."

"How do you know?"

"It was a police car. Didn't you notice?"

Vibeke tries to remember what she saw, but there was nothing about the car or its occupants that made her think specifically of police. He picks up speed again, drumming his fingers on the steering wheel. They're playing a song she likes on the radio, she leans forward to turn up the volume. A bump on the road makes her lose the frequency, the radio hisses and squeals. He pushes a button and turns it off. There's a lull now; she listens to the steady drone of the engine, the hum of the heater. They're probably very conscientious about keeping their vehicles maintained, she thinks, being so dependent on them for getting around. She tries to think of how much they had to drink in the trailer. It can't have been much, she thinks. She puts her head back against the headrest and closes her eyes, her right hand holding the handle of the armrest in the door panel.

The next time she opens her eyes they're turning off the highway, leaving the forest and approaching the outskirts of the town.

Yellow street lamps hang suspended over the asphalt. Staggered rows of dismal, three-storey housing blocks recede back on each side. The gable ends visible from the road have been fitted out with billboards lit up by spotlights. Vibeke thinks the illuminated images with people in them make the place seem populated in the night. They drive past a deserted train station, ice-encrusted and floodlit.

As they near the town center the buildings become taller. Shop windows appear, and neon lights. They pass the hairdressing salon Vibeke's begun to use. The lights are off inside. She pictures the woman who runs the place, the sheen of her neat, short hair, her lips when she talks. She was the one who talked Vibeke into having the stud put in her nose. She made it seem like the obvious thing to do. Her patter about breaking the mold, flouting the rules, putting like and unlike together. Her communicative skills are really quite remarkable, Vibeke considers. My mistake is to think too much when I talk, it slows everything down, repartee just isn't there for me.

She turns her head and looks out the window on the driver's side. She sees a middle-aged couple with a dog on a lead, the man unlocks a gateway door and pushes it open with his shoulder. They drive past too quickly for her to see inside. She thinks of the place they lived before, the rear yard there with the two fine oak trees she could see from the kitchen window. The echo of sounds reverberating between the buildings often woke her up in the mornings; the front door slamming, people standing talking down below. She remembers feeling they belonged together in a way.

The dog begins to whimper now that Jon's just standing there by the door. He doesn't know what it wants, he thinks maybe it's hungry. He whimpers back, thinking it might understand he's got no food. He tries to work out what time it might be if it was eleven at the girl's house. He thinks it must be about half past twelve.

A car comes up the road. Jon hears the sound and sees the headlights before it emerges from the curve of the bend. It's driving slowly. Maybe it's someone who doesn't know the way and now they're looking for someone to ask. He runs down to the road and waves his arms in the air. As the car comes toward him he sees it looks like the red one that sped past when he was walking home.

He pulls in outside an all-night café and lets the engine run. Vibeke feels relieved at not having to talk, the silence between them is suggestive enough on its own. A song verse occurs to her, something about remaining meek, the you inside needs time to speak. Inside the café the young man behind the counter is on the phone, the receiver wedged between his cheek and shoulder. A couple sit eating at a table by the wall, hunched over their plates.

"Smoke?"

"Yes, please," says Vibeke.

He lights up for her, then lights his own. They stare inside again. The man behind the counter is still on the phone, moving his upper body in a series of rhythmic jerks, flicking his wrists, making her think he's listening to music.

"Do you know anywhere?"

"Not really," she says, thinking of the few places she does know, but she's never been here at night before, apart from a theater performance in the church.

They fall silent again.

"Maybe we could ask."

She jabs her cigarette in the direction of the young man inside. He doesn't say anything. He looks like he's thinking. His strong, angular face; his thick hair, curl upon curl. She decides to go in and ask, show some initiative. In a way he's her guest, a visitor to this place where she lives. She opens the car door without looking at him, shuts it quickly behind her and steps over the snow onto the sidewalk. Pressing the curved handle down, she opens the door and goes in.

A strip light floods the tall counter in a glare of light. Apart from that the place is dimly lit by small lamps on all the tables. She's surprised by how loud the music is inside, a disc jockey on some local radio station introduces the next song, it's one they're playing a lot at the moment but she can't remember where she heard it last. She goes up to the counter, finding it hard not to move in time to the music. She places her hands flat on the surface and leans forward. The young man isn't there. She thinks maybe he's gone to the bathroom, or perhaps to the kitchen to fetch some food. There's a smell of burnt coffee from a coffee pot on a hot plate next to some stacked-up cups and saucers. She sways her hips to the music, it feels like ages since she last had a dance. A magazine has been left open on a table behind the counter along with a book. She stretches her neck to see what the book is. She doesn't recognize the title, but the author is an American man.

The category is one she tends to avoid. Next to the table is a swivel chair with tired green upholstery. The radio-cassette player where the music's coming from is also on the table, turned to face whoever sits on the chair. She drums her fingernails on the counter, their deep red against the steel, peering toward the swing doors she assumes lead out to the kitchen. After a moment she turns around and looks out the window at the car. She can't see him very clearly from inside. She glances at the couple eating, there are two dogs lying under their table, and next to the woman's chair is a birdcage with a canary in it. They eat in silence. Vibeke thinks it's as if they can't hear the jaunty voice on the radio or the pounding music that just now comes to an end. Maybe they've been driving all day, she tells herself, and now they're recharging before another shift. The woman shoves her plate away with her food only half eaten and gets a cigarette and lighter out of a packet.

"What would you like?" says a voice behind her. She turns back to the counter. It's not the young man, this one's older. In his fifties, she thinks.

"It was someone else before," she says.

He peers at her and raises his left eyebrow. He puts both his hands down flat on the counter and leans forward. The backs of his hands are covered in dark hair, his forearms too, though the hair on his head is grey. His fingers are thick and stubby.

"Are you having anything or not?"

His voice is calm and steady. Vibeke thinks he sounds tired.

"I was going to ask the young man from before something."

"I see."

There's a lull and she can no longer sense the couple who are eating, she thinks they've probably stopped to hear what she's talking to the man about.

"It doesn't matter," she says.

"I don't suppose it does," says the man. He rearranges some pastries on a plate so they overlap each other in a circle.

Vibeke turns around and goes back toward the heavy glass door where she came in, pushing it open and stepping outside. She breathes the cold air in through her mouth, scuttles back to the car and climbs in.

The car slows down and pulls up next to Jon. He looks at the driver, it's the man with the close-cropped hair. The man looks back at him. The engine idles, puffing its exhaust. Jon feels its warmth against his lower legs.

HE'S TURNED THE ENGINE off but left the ignition on, the heater's running and he's switched the radio back on, the same channel as the one in the café. Now he's asleep. She tries not to slam the door in case she wakes him up. He's put his head back against the headrest. His mouth hangs open, she sees a dark coating on his tongue. From smoking, she guesses, and turns away. She looks out the window on her side. A couple emerge from a place further down the street, they stop, the man puts the woman's head in his hands and bends slightly at the knee as they kiss. Vibeke wonders if there's a coating on her own tongue. She pulls the visor down and looks at herself in the little mirror. She needs to get close up to see properly and shuffles forward to the edge of her seat, balancing awkwardly at an angle. She thinks she can see a dark patch toward the back of her tongue, but it's hard for her to see in such dim light. She investigates with a fingernail, retrieving only slime, and shifts back into her seat. Maybe the place that couple came out is somewhere we can go, she thinks. A warm light seeps out through the door opening. She peers toward it and sees a sign hanging at a right angle to the outside wall. It seems to be a pub of some sort. She turns toward him to wake him up and suggest they have a look. He stares at her with eyes half shut. She wonders if he's been asleep at all, maybe he's been watching her like that all the time. She puts a hand to her hair to see if there's still some bounce in it or if it's collapsed.

The man in the car rolls his window down.

—

"I know the area," says Jon. "If you're lost, that is."

The man smiles. His teeth are small and even. Jon realizes it's a woman, not a man at all.

"Ah, a local."

She keeps smiling as she speaks. She's got an accent, maybe she's from Vestlandet, Jon thinks to himself. He smiles back. He doesn't know what to say, she doesn't seem to be looking for an address after all.

"Hop in," she says with a nod at the empty seat next to her. "It's far too cold to be talking to someone through an open window."

He walks around to the other side and gets in beside her. He glances around the interior. On the back seat is a big, floral cushion and a long white wig. On the floor at his feet is a soft bag made of purple leather. He sits there with his hands on his lap looking straight ahead.

"Aren't boys your age supposed to be in bed by now?"

Her voice is dark and she speaks slowly. It's like she smiles when she's talking, but when Jon looks up at her she goes serious.

"I've locked myself out and there's no one in. My mom's going to be back soon though. She's been baking a birthday cake for me and there was something she'd forgotten to get, so she had to pop out."

"Your birthday soon, is it?"

"Yes, I'm going to be nine tomorrow."

She looks out the windshield at the yellow beam of the headlights in the snow. She clicks her tongue a couple of times, he thinks it's like she doesn't know she's doing it. After a second she leans across the seat where he's sitting and opens the glove compartment.

"There might be some sweets in there somewhere."

She starts rummaging among the pieces of paper, tissues, and some packets of hard candy that seem to be empty. He sees several pairs of sunglasses of different kinds.

"Didn't your mother ever tell you not to go with strangers?"

She rummages on as she speaks.

"Why not?"

"Not everyone's as nice as me."

She looks at him and smiles again. Her teeth are really quite small. He gets an urge to feel his own and compare.

"My mom says everyone's good on the inside."

She rummages still. He studies her. Her clothes are white. Her sweater is made of some kind of soft material, he thinks it looks like the fur of a rabbit. It's a very long sweater, a bit like a dress. She has white tights on, and white lace-up boots. He feels hot and takes his knit cap off.

She slams the glove compartment shut, making him jump.

"Nothing there, I'm afraid."

She looks at him, narrowing her eyes while she thinks.

"We'll go and get some."

She throws the car into gear and swings out into the middle of the road. Jon feels himself thrust into the corner of his seat. She puts her foot down and changes gear. He looks at her hand on the gear lever and thinks how thin her fingers are. He looks at his own hands, they're even smaller than hers. They tingle as the warmth returns to them.

VIBEKE FOLLOWS HIM INSIDE, the smell of his leather jacket filling her nostrils when he stops abruptly and she walks into the back of him. Rather a strong smell, she thinks maybe it's a new jacket. He glances back over his shoulder with a smile. It lifts her up, she feels herself smiling too as she looks around the room. The place is small, the bar cramped and full of customers. On a narrow stage to the left, a couple of steps up from the bar, a band is playing. There are three seating areas to the right of the bar, with brown leather sofas pushed against the wall and wooden chairs facing out. All the seats are taken. Those with nowhere to sit stand with their drinks. The place is so packed it's hard to tell where one group ends and another begins. So this is where people come, she says to herself.

Five girls have sat down on the steps up to the stage. They look like they're having an important discussion. The speakers are right behind them. Vibeke wonders how they can hear each other. She thinks maybe they're deaf and can lip-read, and tries to figure out what they're saying. She can't, and gives up. She wonders what type of music the band is playing. A kind of soft rock perhaps. It's an all-girl band. The bass player's got thick red hair. The singer is short and thin and looks like a child, with a small, round face, big front teeth and black bangs that get in her eyes. The rest of her hair is dreadlocks, all the way down to her waist. They send each other looks as they play, a wry smile at a catchy riff, little nods and gestures to signal the changes. The drummer sits at the back and is ordinary looking. Vibeke thinks if she saw her on the street she'd never believe she played in a band. She looks around, but can't find him. There's a couple having an argument, the girl ranting, the man occasionally managing to get a word in that only sets her off again. She decides not to look. She doesn't want anything to spoil the happiness she feels, the great, unbridled calm inside her. She stays put, standing behind two strapping men with bulging biceps who are sitting on stools, shouting to make themselves heard above the music. She waits for a gap so she can get to the bar and order, trying to make up her mind what she wants, her eyes running down the list on the wall. Something bubbly, she tells herself with a smile, to fit the mood. The men in front of her are talking ice hockey, both seem to be players themselves, they're unhappy with their new coach. Their clothes are the same, red plaid lumberjack shirts and blue jeans. Suddenly one of them twists around and wants to know what's she's staring at. Vibeke is so astonished she can't think of what to say before he's picked up his beer and swivelled around to face her. He rests his elbows on his thighs and gives her a lecture about how he hates being checked out by women standing there ogling, waiting for him to take the initiative; how sick to death he is of eyes all over him, and how she might as well stop gawping, because it doesn't matter how she goes about it, it won't cut any ice with him.

"Hi."

He's standing right behind her, she feels his breath against her hair. He speaks into her ear and makes her smile, picking her up again, restoring the mood, gathering her in. The ice-hockey player turns back to his friend and carries on their conversation as if what he just said to her wasn't an interruption at all but part of a chain of connected events.

"I bumped into some others from the fair."

She turns around and looks up at him. He's sparkling in a way she hadn't seen in the trailer or in the car, he's like a different person. He probably feels more at ease with me now, she thinks, he's starting to relax. She realizes she doesn't know his name and asks.

"Tom," he says. "What's yours?"

"Vibeke."

His eyes wander around the room.

"I need a beer."

"The convenience store shuts at ten," says Jon. "After that there's only the gas station in town."

"Is it far?"

Her dark voice is smooth. Jon thinks she's nice.

"Twenty kilometers."

The heater blasts out hot air. Jon unzips his coat. He unwinds the scarf from around his neck. He sees the big, glassy ring on her middle finger. He wonders what it would look like through the microscope. There must be lots of bacteria on it, he thinks.

They pass under the road lighting as they head along the highway, away from the village. Jon holds his breath for as many lights as he can. He tells himself that as long as he can hold his breath then every light they pass will mean a thousand people get to avoid being tortured. He's read about some methods at the library. For instance, they can hold your head in a bucket of ice-cold water and electrocute you through the tongue. Or else it can be like the picture in the magazine he saw, where they hang you up by the arms and make you pee all down yourself. He tries to imagine how it must feel. The longest he can hold his breath is seven in a row. He thinks maybe he should start practicing so he can manage a bit longer.

The forest around them is dark and dense, the road flat with wide bends. It feels like driving at the bottom of a shaft. Or through a tunnel without a roof, or a deep valley in a model railway landscape.

"What's your name?"

He can tell from her voice she's fed up.

"Jon."

He thinks it's unfair. He never asked to get in. He wasn't pestering her. He only wanted to help, because he thought she was lost.

She drives fast. They enter a bend and the glove compartment drops open. He sees the sunglasses. The nearest pair are big and round, with a thick white rim made of plastic. He gets them out and puts them on. They're far too big for him, he can feel the cold plastic on his cheek. She looks at him, then back at the road. The sunglasses make the beam of the headlights look green. Suddenly he feels sick. His stomach cramps up, his mouth fills with spit. He doesn't think he can keep it in.

"Can you stop?"

"What for?"

"I feel sick."

She drives a bit further then pulls in to the banked-up snow at the roadside. The landscape is flat and open. Jon pulls the door handle and staggers out.

VIBEKE SEES A FACE she recognizes from the Culture Plan presentation, one of the two women from social security. Vibeke had them down as a pair of old hens. Now she's piled on the make-up. Vibeke can see she's with a man, low of stature and thickset, his hair thin and grey. It strikes her they look like they're swing dancing. She laughs. No one else is dancing, there's no room. She sees that the man is drinking water. He must be driving. She looks past them at Tom. He's standing with his back to her at the bar. She can tell he's been served, but he's still chatting with the young barmaid, leaning forward over the counter. The loud music means he has to use his body to make himself understood, and he gestures exaggeratedly with his arms. She supposes he's telling a joke or something. It feels nice, watching him without him knowing. She needs to give him time and space, to be sensitive to the fact that they're two individuals.

"Hi," says the woman from social security. "This is my boyfriend, Evald."

They've come up without her noticing. She didn't think the woman would acknowledge her, they've never spoken before. She's quite drunk. Her boyfriend smiles at Vibeke.

"You're new here," he says.

He bends forward as he speaks, the woman smiles stiffly at Vibeke or something else just beside her. Vibeke nods in return. They must be about sixty. She thinks they're a bit old to be somewhere noisy like this. Or maybe I should think again about older people, she says to herself. She smiles apologetically, indicating the bar with a jab of her thumb and making her way through toward Tom.

The woman tears some paper towels off a roll. He already wiped his mouth on his coat sleeve when he was out of the car, his mouth and face feel dry. He sits there with the paper towels in his hands. He feels the relief of having thrown up, the travel sickness subsiding. She starts the car and pulls away again. She drives slower now.

"You do something with your eyes," she says.

"I know," he says.

They fall silent again. He forgets it shows. But then he gets reminded. All the time, reminded about things. He wishes no one noticed and that what was wrong with him was under his clothes or inside him.

"Well, if you can't help it."

Jon thinks: No, I can't. He stares out at the road in front, feeling the muscle around his eye tighten and release faster than he can think, over and over again. He twists sideways in his seat, putting his chin against his chest and pulling his legs up as far as he can without dirtying the seat with his boots. He closes his eyes and pretends he's the passenger in a spaceship on his way to another planet.

"Don't go to sleep. If I can't sleep at nights, you better not either."

He opens his eyes and looks at her sideways. She's joking, he says to himself. He asks why she can't sleep. She tells him she doesn't know exactly. Something gets in the way, that's all. It feels like something important isn't there when she closes her eyes, she just isn't tired. I sleep fine, says Jon. My mom says anyone can sleep whenever they want, all you've got to do is learn to relax the right way.

He closes his eyes again while she carries on talking. He imagines the squiggles of light he sees behind his eyelids to be undiscovered galaxies. He tries to figure out what to do, whether to land somewhere or be heading into battle, preparing himself for the enemy's onslaught. His neck itches, but it's too much effort to scratch. She hums a song. It distracts him, he tries to ignore it and concentrate on summoning a force. But then his spaceship explodes in a galactic storm and he disintegrates into cosmic dust.

"Great band," says Tom.

She nods. The girl behind the bar puts the beer down in front of her and Vibeke hands her the money. His glass is nearly empty. She looks at him as she sips the froth. It dissolves on her lips. His eyes are big and kind. He's got sleep in the corner of one of them. His mouth is narrow, but it looks so soft and tender.

He turns around and leans back against the bar. He looks down into his beer and a curl of blond hair falls against his cheek with an affirmative bounce, a little yes. She pictures them running toward each other across a city square, a gravel-covered ground, along some disused railway track; he lifts her up and swings her in the air, they laugh together, and the day is bright and soundless. She looks down too; part of her wants to tell him, another part wants to keep it inside. I mustn't spoil the mood with talk, she tells herself.

The floor is wooden, it looks old. It's been sanded down and varnished, a reddish brown. His boots are black with heavy-duty soles. Someone lurches into her, almost knocking her down, and she stumbles toward him, dropping her bag on the floor. Her cheek presses into his sweater, her lower arm forced against his thigh. She can feel

—

93

his penis, hard and stiff inside his pants. She bends down to pick up her bag, and he does too, and they knock their heads together. He lifts her chin and turns her face toward him. His eyes are so close to hers.

"Did you hurt yourself?"

She shakes her head. Her eyes blink and she looks up at the ceiling.

"What's the matter?"

She hears concern.

"It's a lot of things," she says meekly.

She feels herself to be on the verge of telling him, her truth. The stillness. What it means to her to be with him, the way he lifts her up.

"Say again?" he says, lowering his head toward her. "Speak louder."

She tells herself to wait, she wants to hold on to what they've got, she mustn't prick a hole in it. Not this time. I can wait. I'll sheathe us both in speechless intimacy, until we're ready for the abruptness of words.

"It's the smoke, that's all," she says, looking at him, trying to tell him what she wants to say with her eyes. "I'm not used to so much smoke."

Jon is woken by warm air against his face. It smells nice and he opens his eyes. The woman in the white clothes is leaning over him, is almost on top of him; it's her breath that feels so warm. He senses the car has come to a halt, it's dark everywhere, so dark the snow looks luminous. His eyes adjust. He thinks to himself the darkness is actually quite light.

"You're drooling on the seat."

—

94

Her voice sounds tired. He feels stiff, as if he's been asleep for some time. His mouth is dry. He uses the paper towels scrunched up in his hand to wipe his cheek and chin. The spit feels cold against his skin.

"I don't normally," he says. "Have we been stopped long?"

He thinks to himself that if they haven't then he won't have said much in his sleep, he talks in his sleep sometimes and he doesn't want her to hear things he might say. He tries not to blink.

"I don't know."

She takes a cigarette out of a packet on the dashboard, lights up and leans back against the headrest. She blows the smoke out in rings while staring out at the road in front. The heater hums. He imagines they're sitting inside a snow globe, Vibeke gave him an old one from when her mother was a little girl, he keeps it on his bedside table, and when he shakes it white flakes of something that looks like snow fall on the little houses inside.

"A quarter of an hour, something like that. Want a smoke?"

He wonders what she means, she knows how old he is. At school they say you die from it. He told Vibeke, she said some of us have to die so others can live and enjoy, or something like that.

"My mom smokes," he says.

"It makes your hair fall out," says the woman, pointing at her fuzzy hair with a smile.

"Not my mom's. Hers is really long and black, it goes all the way down to her belly button." *I've got the hair of a horse, Jon.*

He wonders if you get less smoke inside you if you only breathe

—

through your mouth and keep your nostrils closed. He's sure it wouldn't taste of anything if that was what you did.

"She wears a little diamond in her nose too, doesn't she, your mom?" the woman says.

"Yes," says Jon. "It's not a real diamond though, it just looks like one. She says she's going to buy a real one when she gets rich. Do you know my mom?"

"I'm psychic," she says.

"What does that mean?"

"It's when you see people in your mind that you don't know, that sort of thing. It's secret."

He doesn't believe her, but doesn't want to say so.

She takes a drag of the cigarette then hands it to him. He reaches out and scissors his fingers around the filter. She guides his hand with hers. He puts the cigarette between his lips and sucks. He can smell her fingers, he thinks she must use lotion of some kind. He exhales, blowing the smoke out onto his hand and hers. The air greys in front of his eyes. He expects to cough but doesn't. He thought it would make him choke. Is he a smoker now? She removes her hand, studying his reactions. He takes a puff while she lights up another. She leans back in her seat, he does the same. They stare out ahead, through the windshield at the snow-covered road. There haven't been any cars since he woke up. He holds the cigarette between his index finger and thumb, and thinks one day he'll take his driving test.

THE VOCALIST IN THE BAND mumbles something into the microphone in a deep voice. They're finished for the night. The audience clap and the girls start packing their gear. Someone puts a CD on. The music is soft and gentle, Vibeke thinks it must be jazz of some sort. She watches the girl with the red hair as she puts her bass away in a case lined with sheepskin. She looks at Tom, his eyes are closed as he sips his beer. He's still standing back against the bar. She asks him what he's thinking about. He doesn't seem to notice she's speaking to him. She angles forward, stretching onto her tiptoes, and asks him again, her lips to his ear.

"Summer," he says without opening his eyes.

The thought makes her feel buoyant. She thinks about it too, they've known nothing but snow since they moved here. She wonders what it's like when it's warm, when the fells are streaked with color and the sun shines. She imagines sitting outside under the shade of a tree. She studies him and finds she likes him with his eyes shut too, immersed in his own world. He could sit in the other chair. With glasses on, she thinks, most likely he wears glasses to read. Round ones with wire rims. She wonders if he reads quickly or slowly. She feels an urge to ask. She thinks the speed at which a person reads says something about the kind of rhythm they possess, the way they are in life.

Her attention is distracted by some people leaving. They've left the door open while they say their goodbyes and give each other hugs.

—

Someone closes it. Vibeke thinks it'll be open again in a second. Then there he is all of a sudden, the young man from the café. He leans up to a young girl with blond hair and says something that makes her laugh. Vibeke thinks she can't be more than seventeen.

The woman from social security clutches her boyfriend's hand. They bump into the blond-haired girl on their way out. She doesn't seem to notice. A lot of people left when the band stopped playing, but there's still quite a few hanging around. The boyfriend holds the door for her. Vibeke sees her shudder as she goes out into the cold, as if her thinking had lagged behind and left her unprepared. She thinks of their own drive home, how good it feels to be going home with someone instead of alone. She looks at Tom leaning against the bar. His eyes are still closed. He breathes calmly through his nose, inhaling deeply. She admires the way he can relax. He looks almost like he's asleep. She wishes she could lie in a bed and watch him.

"What are we waiting for?" she says, and feels a reflex in her hand wanting to smooth his hair. She stops herself, not wishing to encroach on his space. Never encroach.

"Can't we go now?"

Her voice is fuller than before, a dark and sensual resonance drawn from her diaphragm. He turns back around to face the bar, a half-liter glass in front of him on a beer mat advertizing a local big band.

"I still need to get this down."

He raises his glass to her with a glance and a little nod. It's still half-full. She thinks his eyes look glazed. Perhaps he's not all there. He takes a sip and licks his upper lip, looking over her shoulder at the people leaving.

—

The music's been turned down. The girl behind the bar is busy putting clean glasses away in the racks above their heads. They chink together. Someone scrapes a chair. The stool beside him is vacated. She hoists herself up and sits down.

Smoke smells different when it's your own, Jon thinks. He turns his head slightly and looks at the woman with the short hair. She looks like a man again now that she's got her mouth closed, her jawbone is more prominent. He sees her cheek muscles tighten and release, tighten and release, like a pulse. He tries doing the same to see what it feels like, clenching his teeth and letting go. He's not quite sure he's doing it right. It makes his jaw tired, and he makes a face to loosen up. She turns her head and looks at him, tightening and releasing. She doesn't know she's doing it, he says to himself. He thinks of a wildlife program he saw on TV about lizards in the desert, a lot of them kept doing this thing with their neck, he remembers the voice saying it was an instinct, something they did before pouncing on their prey. He closes his eyes so he wouldn't see. He hears the hum of the heater. He decides to count how many constellations he knows. He counts them quietly. When he can't think of any more he opens his eyes.

She looks out the window on his side. She's stopped clenching now, he thinks she just looks tired again. He turns around to see what she's looking at. There's nothing there, only forest.

"A deserted road, in the middle of the forest, in the middle of the night."

She looks out at the trees as she speaks, shifting her gaze toward him as her words trail off.

"The town's just a bit further on, there's a gas station by the turn-off," says Jon. "It doesn't matter though. My mum's probably home by now."

"Mommy, mommy," she mocks, in a voice like a child's.

He thinks about one of the music videos he saw at the girl's house. The lady who was the singer was in a car with the man driving, it was a foreign country, an island in Italy perhaps. They drove all afternoon and it was starting to get dark when this big house came into view at the top of a hill. The road got worse and the car nearly got stuck, there was a close-up of one of the wheels spinning in the mud. Eventually, they made it around the final bend up to the house and outside there was a battered sign saying *Hotel*. The place was creepy, there was no one around and no lights on anywhere. But then when the man and the singer lady carried their suitcases into the reception some people in uniform came out to meet them. That was the end.

"Have people got snowmobiles here?" the woman asks.

"Yes," says Jon.

"Why don't they use them then? You'd think it'd be more practical," she says. "I haven't seen a single one."

"I don't know," says Jon.

"What's the point of having them if they don't get used?"

He thinks about the snowmobiles he's seen parked outside the houses. Usually they're under tarps, and always on the side facing the forest. Their owners put one foot on the running board and their other knee on the seat, then they pull the starter cord and drive off, half crouching, half standing, into the trees and away. Sometimes in the night he gets woken up by the sound of a snowmobile starting up and setting off, or another coming back, returning home. The first few times he thought the sound they made was like a machine gun.

"They do get used, a lot of people use them in fact. But we haven't got one. Vibeke doesn't like being out in the snow. I have skates though," says Jon. "And I know a man who won the Kalottløpet before the war. His skates are in a box in the basement."

"ALL RIGHT, LET'S GO," says Tom.

He strides toward the door, Vibeke feels she ought to have gone to the bathroom. The room's almost empty. The house lights have been switched on. She sees the walls are unevenly painted and grubby, there's dust all along the chair rail. Tom steps out, peering into the street as he holds the door for her. She clenches her coat at the collar, checking with her other hand to make sure she's remembered her gloves and her bag.

Some other people follow them out, she hears the door close again and footsteps as they trudge away.

The cold feels rough against her face. The snow is heaped up at the curbsides. Across the road, a van's been left hemmed in by the snow plow.

She pauses at the silence. Listen, she wants to say, listen to how quiet it is. She looks up at the sky. She can no longer see the stars. It must have clouded over. He walks toward the car. She sees his hair isn't cut straight at the neck.

"I need the bathroom," she says.

Tom stops. He breathes out heavily. She turns to go back inside but finds the door locked. She knocks.

He stands back and looks down the road. His shoulders are slightly rounded. She feels the cold against her throat. A car that's been parked facing the sidewalk backs out into the road. The white reversing lights go out and it pulls away. It's a police car, one of the old square ones.

The girl from behind the bar unlocks the door, holding it open with her arm outstretched. She asks what they want. Vibeke says she needs the bathroom, she forgot to go and they've got a drive ahead of them. The girl nods before she's finished explaining, and steps aside for her to get past. Vibeke senses her looking at Tom.

Think ten nice thoughts, she tells herself as she sits down on the toilet. The tiles on the floor are a pattern of alternating green and blue. The wastebasket next to the sink is full to the brim, the floor littered with paper towels. Someone's blotted their lipstick on one, she can see the print of their lips. She brushes her hair again. It frames her face in the mirror. Not bad, she thinks, and smiles. Not bad at all.

When she comes back out, Tom and the girl are standing at the corner of the bar, each with a little glass in front of them, talking softly. Vibeke stands on the narrow stage where the band was playing. Make him turn and see me. *You look gorgeous.* She can't hear what they're saying. She steps down and goes up to them. The girl says hi and asks if she'd like something. Vibeke shakes her head. She feels a bit nauseous, she wonders if it's too much smoking again. She lingers at Tom's side, listening to the girl telling him about an ice-fishing competition at a nearby lake. The Storvannet. Vibeke has heard about it at work. You can't see it from the highway, but apparently it's just on the other side. There's a particular spot where cars are often parked, she thinks it must be there. Tom throws in comments about jigs and tackle, various techniques. She didn't know he was interested.

She looks up at the ceiling. There's a shiny fan in the middle. It's not moving. The planks are painted brown, with black and metal trim.

———

The woman with the short hair has fallen asleep. Her mouth is closed. Jon thinks maybe her teeth are false. He's not tired anymore and he doesn't know what to do now on his own. *I'm closing the door now. You're a big boy, the dark's nothing to be scared of. What you're scared of is inside you. You've got to choose, Jon, decide where to invest your energy. If you want to be scared, you will be. If not, all you have to do is think of something else. I'm closing the door now. Sleep tight.* He stares out at the forest. His eyes are used to the dark now, the trees at the roadside stand out clearly. It feels like he hasn't blinked for some time. Maybe it's wearing off, he thinks. Maybe it's going away right at this moment. He sees a pattern of indentations in the snow by the car. He thinks they must be animal tracks.

Vibeke leaves them to it and goes outside, pulling the door shut behind her as she steps out.

The street lights have gone out, they switch them off in the middle of the night here. Only the neon signs illuminate the dark, the shop windows, an advertising sign over at the bank. She thinks of how different everywhere looks in the lightless hours. She read about it once in a book, she can't remember the title. She thinks if she'd only ever been here at night and came back in the day she probably wouldn't recognize it.

She pulls her gloves out of her coat pocket and puts them on before wrapping her scarf snugly around her neck. I'll leave him alone for a bit, she thinks, that way he'll see how generous I am. He can have all the space he needs with me. We can't be all things to each other, no one can. I'm showing him more of me now than if I'd stayed.

She goes toward the car. The wind has started to blow, the snow whips along the ground.

At first she thinks the car door's locked, but then when she presses more firmly and pulls harder on the handle it opens.

The glove compartment drops open again, he stops it with his left hand so the noise won't wake her up. He feels hungry. He often gets up to eat in the night. The light's always on outside his room, shining up the stairs. He wonders if Vibeke forgets to switch it off. He cuts himself some bread and spreads something on before putting everything back in its place, sweeping the crumbs off the counter into his hand and dropping them in the sink. Then he sits down at the kitchen table and looks out at the road while he eats. He especially likes to sit there when it's snowing; he'll put the radio on low then and listen to the night shows, the requests, the soft, mellow voices.

He looks at her. She's still asleep. He finds some receipts and some documents from an insurance company, some papers with the funfair's logo in the top right-hand corner. There's a postcard too. It shows a green entrance door with red flowers all around it, in the window is a yellow vase with a single stalk. On the other side there's some writing in a language he can't understand. At the back of the glove compartment he finds a cell phone. He takes it out and flips it open. He thinks about calling home. He thinks about Vibeke, she's bound to be home by now; the cake will be ready, maybe she's already gone to bed. If he calls he'll wake her up. She doesn't like being on the phone. *I like to see who I'm talking to.* If it rings in the afternoon she gets him to answer. Afterwards she'll ask who it was, what their voice sounded like, what they said when he told them she wasn't in. Sometimes she'll wait a bit, then call them back. *Don't let others govern your time.* He closes the phone again and puts it back. She'd only wonder who it was, she probably thinks I'm in bed asleep.

There are some coins in the glove compartment too, but he doesn't have the courage to take them in case the woman wakes up.

IT FEELS WARMER INSIDE the car than out, it must be the wind. Then immediately she senses the cold. It doesn't come creeping, the way it's supposed to, it's just there. Encasing her. She feels like she's freezing to the bone, yet tells herself to stick it out and wait until he comes. Here I am, near and serene. Facing away from the bar entrance she can't see if he's coming or not. She closes her eyes and forces herself to sit back and relax.

She wonders what he's trying to say by making her wait. Maybe he's testing her, trying to find her limit. Something he can relate to. But he can relate to me the way I am, she thinks to herself. What's wrong with using language? She can feel the thought, a build-up of pressure above her left eyebrow. She locates it precisely with her finger and massages for a moment before the tenderness makes her stop.

She doesn't hear him coming until a second or two before he opens the door. It startles her. She'd expected having to wait some time, but now he's back already.

He looks at her, glancing then by turn at the dashboard, the back seats, the floor, her feet, the gear lever, the pedals. As if he's making sure everything's still there, she thinks.

He says nothing, but gets in and starts patting his pockets. Vibeke recalls him doing the same thing when they first met at the fair. In a way, she knows him already; she sees him from an angle from which he can never see himself. He arches off the seat and feels in his back pockets without finding what he's looking for, and sits down again.

He pats the breast pocket of his shirt one more time under his sweater and finds the car keys there. She doesn't say anything either. She closes her eyes again as he turns the ignition and the car starts. The heater blasts air. He reverses out into the road, thrusts the car into gear and drives back the way they came. Vibeke sees the lights in the café have been turned off as they go past.

He swerves through a roundabout and she tips toward him, stopping herself with a hand against his seat, then straightening up.

CLOSING THE GLOVE COMPARTMENT, he finds a yellow candy in the groove. It must have fallen out of a packet, it has dust stuck to it. He puts it in his mouth and sucks. It tastes of butter. He thinks of a rhyme he learned with corresponding hand movements, drumming different fingers in a certain pattern as fast as you can. It's best against a hard surface, but he uses his thigh so it doesn't make too much noise. After a while he tries with both hands at once, only it's slower that way. He concentrates on speeding it up, then feels something press against his left temple.

Tom turns the headlights on full. He whistles to himself for a bit, tosses a packet of chewing gum onto the dashboard and asks if she wants some. She shakes her head. They've already left the town behind. He tells her about something he and a couple of the guys from the fair did a while back, it was just before closing, some girls were on one of the rides, but instead of stopping it after the usual time they kept it going and wouldn't let them off. He laughs.

"What are you playing at?"

Her voice sounds forceful and commanding, Jon can hardly tell it's hers. He stops drumming and looks up at her. She's sitting with her head back the way she was when she was asleep, her eyes are narrow slits looking askance at him. He says it's just a game he's practicing. She doesn't say anything. Jon tells her how hard it is to do with both hands, and demonstrates. When he's finished he wants to know what she thinks. She stares out at the road in front of them. His eyes follow hers and look out.

The landscape opens briefly as they approach the steep hill before the long, flat stretch through the forest. Vibeke knows the way now. It feels shorter every time. It's as if Tom is invigorated by the sight of the seemingly endless ribbon of road; he speeds up. The beam of the headlights is a wide cone of white in the dark, it's like the road ahead keeps expanding. *The Expanding World*, that science book on her shelf. She hasn't read it yet, there's always a novel that's more appealing. She must mention it to Tom sometime. When it comes to modern physics she feels completely blank, but it seems very interesting.

Jon is blinded by the glare of the oncoming vehicle, he glances away, then peers back through screwed-up eyes. He can see it's got big wheels and is higher up off the road than a normal car. An army vehicle, he thinks to himself. In a few seconds we'll be caught in its lights and be discovered. He ducks down in his seat and puts his head against his knees. The invaders are here and their spotlights have got deadly lasers in them. She asks what he's doing. He doesn't have time to answer. The car flashes past.

"Did you see that?" says Tom.

Vibeke asks what he means.

"That car we just passed."

"Yes," says Vibeke, wondering why he sounds so irritable all of a sudden. "I don't think it was the police though."

"But there was someone in it, didn't you see?"

"Maybe they just wanted to be on their own for a bit. Maybe they were listening to some classical music."

—

She looks at him. He stares stiffly out at the road in front. She feels a tenderness for him, he seems so burdened. She wishes he'd let her help.

Jon hears the vehicle fade into the distance. They sit quite still, as if they're both listening. The woman with the short hair spits some words out between her lips:

"The stupid fuck."

She lights up a cigarette and takes a series of long, deep pulls. Her movements are calm and measured, but her hands are shaking slightly. The car fills with smoke again.

Abruptly she turns the ignition, grips the steering wheel with both hands and turns the car around on the road. A wheel spins in the snow before finding purchase.

Vibeke looks out at the dark forest, the curving road ahead. She tries to think how long it'll be before they're back. Tom sings a song with a seemingly endless number of verses. After each chorus he strikes his index finger twice against the steering wheel. She studies his body, his face. There's a little fleck of dried toothpaste in the corner of his mouth, she hadn't noticed until now. She tries to think back to when he brushed his teeth, it must have been in the trailer just before they left. She feels tired in a nice sort of way and feels an urge to snuggle up to him, to fall asleep and wake up with someone warm.

"So, what does the future hold for you?" she asks.

"If only I knew," he says.

"I mean, in most books there's a chapter two, a continuation of the story that's started."

"I hope so."

"What about this story, tonight? How does the next chapter go?"

Tom sighs. He opens his mouth, then shuts it again. Then he says:

"You know as well as I do you can't continue something that never started."

A silence ensues. Vibeke wishes she hadn't asked. She's been too direct again and he feels pressured, invaded. It annoys her, she'd been doing so well lately recognizing people's boundaries. Sometimes though you've got to take a chance and run the risk.

"Things can be going on inside you without you even knowing. A chance encounter can set things in motion and you don't always realize until afterwards that something has happened and you're changed. You must always be humble and take into account that you perhaps haven't got the full picture."

She sees him clench his teeth. There's something untamed about him, she thinks to herself. He lacks impulse control. The way he stayed behind to talk to that girl in the bar, even though he knew she was sitting there in the cold waiting for him. Maybe he's unbalanced. Maybe he's working on keeping a hold on himself, and the control he thereby achieves is something he needs to cling to. When she thinks of it like that the opposites inside him seem to be reconciled. Mental disorder and intellectual capacity are often closely connected, she thinks of the books in the trailer. Now he's travelling around with the fair as part of some rehabilitation program. The woman in the white wig was a bit weird too.

Her eyes follow the marker poles at the side of the road, the even spaces between them forming a rhythm in her mind.

She feels alone and strong.

—

The woman with the short hair tells him to sit up and stop fooling around. Jon looks at her; the way she smokes, hard, snappy drags. She hasn't asked if he wants one. Maybe she really is a man, Jon thinks to himself, her nose is a bit big. He tries to see if there's a bulge in her pants. He can't tell one way or another, her white sweater covers her thighs. He can't see her titties either, he thinks if she's got any they must be pretty small. She asks him what he's staring at. Or rather *he* asks, Jon thinks to himself. "Nothing," he replies, and looks down at his hands, his fingers, comparing them to those on the steering wheel. He can hardly recognize them as his own.

They come out of the bend into the lit-up stretch of road before the turn-off to the village. To the right she can see the lights of the fair, the garlands of light bulbs, red, yellow, green, blue, purple, orange, sagging arcs against the darkness of the sky. Like the bead necklaces she had when she was little. She remembers the marbles all of a sudden and puts a hand in her pocket to feel them. They're not cold anymore. She takes one out and slips it behind her into the crack of the seat without him noticing; a small part of her will now be with him, even if he doesn't know. Maybe he'll find it one day and remember her.

They pass the council offices. Her own office faces the other side, her window can't be seen from the road. He slows down and pulls in.

"Tell me which way and I'll drop you off."

She pauses.

He revs the engine.

"Just follow the road," she says, softly so as not to provoke him. "It's not far."

JON PRETENDS HE'S PRESSED back in his seat by the sheer force of acceleration as the craft thrusts away into space. He looks up at her, the muscles of her jaw tightening and releasing again. He looks back at the road, at the beam of the headlights against the white mantle of snow; he thinks of the car as a robot, and no matter what happens the robot is programed to find its way home.

Vibeke stares out the window as they rumble past the supermarket and the bus stop. She glances at the speedometer; it's not because he's driving that slow, it just feels like it because they were going so fast before. Her eyes look out beyond him at the lightless houses, the cars parked in the driveways, the curtains drawn in all the windows. She sees a dog, stock-still at a front door, staring up at the handle, wanting in. Something tells her it's been waiting for some time.

"Here we are," she says, pointing as they approach.

He pulls up and leaves the engine running. She looks across at the windows. The living room is faintly lit, she knows it's the light on in the hall. Apart from that, the windows are all dark. She thinks how empty they look, her plants always die on her. She hasn't bought any curtain material yet, blaming the limited choice, but the truth is she doesn't much care for curtains, they blur the lines of the room.

"It's nicer inside than it looks from here."

She isn't afraid of him.

He says nothing, but sits there, slightly inclined toward the front of his seat, with his head lowered, staring at the steering wheel. He turns and looks at her.

"Should be getting back, get some sleep before the day starts."

She looks at him with eyes she feels gleam with consideration and respect. Most likely he's got more inhibitions than seem apparent. She studies him, her eyes passing over his face one last time, the thickness of his hair.

"Take good care," she says. "Promise?"

She emphasizes each word to make him feel she means it, that it's not just something she says.

He smiles faintly.

She unfastens her seat belt, allowing it to snap back as she lets go. She finds the latch and pulls the black plastic handle back. The lock releases with a click, the cold air assailing her calves and thighs as she opens the door and swings her legs out. The vehicle's elevation obliges her to slide downward until her feet reach the ground. She twists around and leans back inside, picking up her bag from the leg space. He looks out at the road in front.

She closes the door, though not hard enough. He leans across, opens it again and shuts it properly. Their eyes meet before he leans back. He puts the car into gear, it rolls gently forward then pulls away as he puts his foot down.

Vibeke wanders toward the house. She stops and looks back in the direction he drove off, his red rear lights leaving their rose-colored trail in the snow. He heads north without turning around, as if he knows the road leads back to the highway again. Maybe he's been here before after all. She can't figure him out. His eyes were so intelligent.

She opens her bag and rummages for a moment, her fingers icy cold. Then she remembers she put the key in her coat pocket. She finds it and gets it out.

THEY TURN IN AT the council offices, following the road through the little wood to the community center and the sports ground. It's not a real wood, Jon thinks to himself, just a few birch trees, that's all. The fairground lights are still on, their colors shining brightly in the dark night. Jon thinks it looks like a colony from outer space camped out on Earth, the lights are a shield of death rays protecting them from intruders. The woman backs in next to a pile of snow, then switches off the engine and the headlights, leaving the heater on. She lights another cigarette and exhales calmly while staring at the lights. She looks sad, Jon thinks. The light bulbs fleck the snow with color. He thinks of how the flecks can be seen but if you try to touch them they vanish.

"Let me smoke this, then I'll take you home. Okay?"

She smiles faintly. Jon thinks she looks just as sad when she smiles. He swivels around and peers through the rear window. More birch trees, here and there some fir. A carrier bag and some empty beer bottles lie strewn around a shallow pit in the snow, its edges blackened by fire.

Vibeke drapes her coat over the chair by the phone, goes into the bathroom and sits down on the toilet. She leans forward, her elbows against her knees. Life is so wonderful and strange, she thinks to herself with a smile and shakes her head.

Another car turns in at the council offices, passing between the council building and the community center. It's a big four-wheel drive

—

like the one they saw on the road before they turned back to the village. It rolls up next to the fairground entrance and stops. The driver switches off the headlights and engine. A man climbs out with a black leather jacket on and a head full of curly blond hair. He shuts the door behind him, opens and shuts it again. He lingers for a moment, at one point turning his head so Jon feels he's looking straight at them. Then after a second he walks away. He steps lightly, Jon thinks. His walk's nearly a skip.

The man goes in through the entrance, disappearing from view among the rides, dissolving into the dark.

The woman stubs her cigarette out in the little compartment. It's full of old ends and ash. She glances at Jon out of the corner of her eye, hardly turning her head. She doesn't want to look at me, he thinks. He feels with his hand to see if he's been drooling again. He can sense he's blinking. He tries not to. There's no spit from his mouth.

She says she thinks his mom's home again now. She can feel it, she says, she's almost certain.

"Do you want me to drop you off?"

Jon thinks he can tell from her voice she doesn't want to.

"I'll walk," he says. "It's not far and I know the way."

"As long as you're sure?" she says.

Jon says he'll be fine and gets out. She leans over and locks his door, then gets out herself and locks her own.

For a moment everything is still.

The snow creaks under their feet as they walk from the car. She thanks him for the company, scrutinizing him for a second, her head tilted slightly to the side, before turning around and walking away

—

through the lit-up entrance in the same direction as the man, across the deserted fairground. The white wig is in her hand, its long hair trailing on the ground as she disappears behind a trailer.

He stamps his feet, a series of dull, echoing thuds. When he stops, the silence is even clearer. He wonders if sounds are bigger in the cold. And if it was cold enough whether sound could make the planet explode.

HE CUTS BETWEEN THE council offices and the supermarket, following the path that's been trampled in the snow. He pretends he's just landed on Earth. All the people are dead. Killed by death rays. He hurries between the buildings, scurrying in the direction of the road. The tips of his ears are cold. He must have left his knit cap somewhere, he had it when he came out. He puts his hands to his ears to warm them up. He forces himself not to see the trees, the forest; whenever he's on his own it's like there's always someone standing there.

Vibeke goes into the bedroom. She sets the alarm clock, flipping open the little cover to set the switch while trying not to look at what time it is. Knowing would only keep her awake, thinking about how soon she has to be up again. She puts the alarm clock down on the floor. The blind is already down, it's been down all day. She undresses with her eyes closed, as if to lull herself to sleep. She pulls the duvet aside and gets into bed, tucking it tight around her body and legs. She tries to focus her mind on slow, deep breathing, a technique she learned on a course she was on with her previous job. The trick is to consciously relax, starting with the toes then moving upwards through the body section by section. By the time she gets to her head she already feels drowsy. She sees the brown eyes of the engineer from the building department.

Jon pauses outside the house where the girl lives. He looks up at the window he thinks must be the room he looked into from the doorway upstairs. The curtains are open, but there's no light on. The lamp above the bed must have been switched off. He glances around then looks again, but there's no one looking back at him.

On the other side of the road a path leads past the houses into the forest. A hundred meters along the path there's a slope with floodlights put up. The smaller children play there on their baby skis, they pretend it's real skiing. Jon was there not long ago with one of the boys from his class, the boy had borrowed a sledge trailer from someone's snowmobile without asking. There must have been ten of them on it, hurtling down the hill until they got stuck or crashed, tumbling out into the snow, its icy crystals penetrating under their collars and scarves. Maybe someone's there now, he thinks. He decides to go up the bank around the back of the houses and see. If I do that, he tells himself, mom will be home when I get back.

THE COLD NIPS AT his ears and forehead. He stands on top of the bank behind the houses and peers toward the forest. Ahead, the floodlights illuminate the slope. He thinks he hears voices, but there's no one there to see.

The snow under the lights is amber and bronze, inkier in the dips where the shadows fall. It doesn't look at all frightening. The forest all around is still. Jon thinks if he goes to the floodlights he'll have won for doing something he was scared of.

He picks his way between the footprints and ski tracks, treading only where the snow is untouched. He breathes a rhythm to sound like a train.

He looks up and sees he's only halfway. Perhaps it's further than he thought. He tells himself he mustn't look before the ground starts sloping upwards.

The last bit is steep, but he wants to save the view until he's gotten to the top. His legs are numb. The wind creeps under his coat. His old one had a drawstring he could pull tight, but this one's different.

At the top he turns around and looks out over the village. The street lights form a squashed circle, twinkling in the dark. It seems so far away. He finds it odd that he should live there, so very strange it looks, a ring of lights on another planet. He wants to go home. He's freezing cold. The bitter air bites at his skin, his face is stiff, his fingers and thighs. He needs to go home now. He wishes he could blink and be there. Suppose he can't find his way and gets lost? In the floodlights on top of the hill he suddenly feels exposed, he could be seen by anyone, a dark fleck moving about against the white. He mustn't turn around. Beyond the hill the path winds off into the forest and continues up onto the fell. If he turns around now they'll grab him and snatch him away. He'd never get back to the road ever again.

He goes back down again, cautiously, so as not to slip and fall where the ice has formed. He doesn't turn around, but proceeds calmly. You musn't show them you're scared. That's when they come for you, when they know you're scared. Luckily they can't see him blinking in the dark. He makes the train sound in his mind, steady and strong, and feels his pee seep against his thigh. He presses on regardless so no one can tell.

Reaching the foot of the bank on the other side he starts to run, to the safety of the flat road. His legs won't go fast enough, he stumbles in the hollow of a footprint and falls headlong, reaching his hands out in front of him to break the impact. It feels like someone's clutching at his legs, he squirms away, his fingers clawing at the snow. He scrabbles to his feet and staggers out into the road, stumbling once more, only now it doesn't matter, now he's safe.

He brushes himself down and walks straight home.

As soon as he comes around the corner it jumps out at him: the car's not there. He stops. What's he going to do? She must have had an accident like he thought. Now she's lying dead in the road. And he'll be put in a home. He tries to imagine what it'll be like.

It must be after midnight now, he thinks. Today's his birthday. Now he's nine years old.

—

An accident on her way home from the village and it's all his fault.

If it hadn't been his birthday everything would have stayed the same. He promises himself that if everything can just be all right he'll never think of birthdays ever again. He doesn't need presents. He needs to stop blinking, to keep practicing holding his breath.

He walks on, up the driveway to the front door.

The metal of the door handle is covered in frost, he feels an urge to put his tongue to it. He thinks of what would happen, the skin, the blood. He heard someone talk about it at school. He decides not to. He holds his breath and listens for Vibeke's car. She can still be coming, maybe some problem held her up.

He can't hear anything, not even from the highway. He was freezing cold a minute ago. His toes and feet, his calves and thighs, his bottom, his cheeks, mouth, and hands, every part of him was ice. Now he can't feel it anymore. He kicks at a pile of snow he cleared from the driveway, but nothing happens apart from a few little lumps that dislodge and roll to the ground. He picks one up. It feels warm in his hand. He bites into it and crunches it between his teeth.

He sits down. He feels tired, as if he's been playing basketball all day, his arms and legs are heavy as logs. Perhaps it won't be long before she's back. He puts his ear to the ground and listens for the sound. Even from a distance he knows the sound of her car.

He closes his eyes. He sees the car in his mind's eye, intact and immaculate. He sees the wheels as they roll through the snow.

The wheels rolling on tracks in the snow. Because it's a train, he says to himself. The trains go where the road is, through the village, with shiny red engines. Didn't she say she'd be coming on the train and would take him with her? That they'd go away together?

And isn't that the whistle he hears, a short, crisp blast? It is, it's the whistle. Now it won't be long and the train will be here.

He stretches out on his tummy, settling into sleep. Inside his head everything is dark and big and still.

He'll wait for her here.

archipelago books

is a not-for-profit literary press devoted to
promoting cross-cultural exchange through innovative
classic and contemporary international literature
www.archipelagobooks.org